The Sunny Side of the Street

Marshall P. Wilder

Alpha Editions

This edition published in 2024

ISBN : 9789364732338

Design and Setting By
Alpha Editions
www.alphaedis.com
Email - info@alphaedis.com

As per information held with us this book is in Public Domain. This book is a reproduction of an important historical work. Alpha Editions uses the best technology to reproduce historical work in the same manner it was first published to preserve its original nature. Any marks or number seen are left intentionally to preserve its true form.

Contents

PREFACE .... - 1 -

I SUNSHINE AND FUN .... - 2 -

II SUNNY MEN OF SERIOUS PRESENCE .... - 6 -

III AT THE WHITE HOUSE AND NEAR IT .... - 12 -

IV STORY-TELLING AS AN ART .... - 21 -

V ACTORS' JOKES .... - 27 -

VI A SUNNY OLD CITY .... - 35 -

VII MY FIRST TRIP TO LONDON .... - 42 -

VIII EXPERIENCES IN LONDON .... - 50 -

IX "LUCK" IN STORY-TELLING .... - 57 -

X JOURNALISTS AND AUTHORS .... - 64 -

XI THE UNEXPECTED .... - 72 -

XII SUNSHINE IN SHADY PLACES .... - 83 -

XIII "BUFFALO BILL" .... - 91 -

XIV THE ART OF ENTERTAINING .... - 98 -

XV IN THE SUNSHINE WITH GREAT PREACHERS ....- 103 -

XVI THE PRINCE OF WALES (*Now King Edward VII*)..- 110 -

XVII SIR HENRY IRVING ....- 116 -

XVIII LONDON THEATRES AND THEATRE-GOERS..- 124 -

XIX TACT ....- 130 -

XX ADELINA PATTI..- 139 -

XXI SOME NOTABLE PEOPLE ....- 147 -

XXII HUMAN NATURE...- 154 -

XXIII SUNNY STAGE PEOPLE ....- 160 -

XXIV SUNSHINE IS IN DEMAND ....- 166 -

XXV "BILL" NYE ....- 170 -

XXVI SOME SUNNY SOLDIERS....................................- 175 -

XXVII SOME FIRST EXPERIENCES ....- 185 -

PREFACE

In this little volume are offered recollections of the sunny side of many people. I have plucked blossoms from the gardens of humor and pathos, which lie side by side, and in weaving them into a garland, claim only as my own the string that binds them together.

I
SUNSHINE AND FUN

The Sunny Side of the Street.—Jests and Jesters.—The Force of a Joke.—Lincoln's Way.—Kings and Their Joke-Makers.—As they do it in Persia and Ireland.—"Chestnuts."—Few Modern Jesters but no End of Jokers.—Entertainers and Their Ways.

I live on the sunny side of the street; shady folks live on the other. I always preferred the sunshine, and have tried to put other people there, if only for an hour or two at a time, even if I had to do it after sunset from a platform under the gaslight, with my name billed at the door as entertainer.

As birds of a feather flock together, it has been my good fortune to meet thousands of other people on the sunny side of the street. In this volume I shall endeavor to distribute some of the sunshine which these fine fellows unloaded on me.

Nature has put up many effective brands of concentrated sunshine in small packages; but the best of these, according to all men of all countries, is the merry jest. As far back as history goes you will find the jest, also the jester. The latter was so important that kings could not get along without him. Some kings more powerful than any European sovereign is to-day are remembered now only by what their jesters said.

All these jesters are said to have been little people. I am doubly qualified to claim relationship with them, for I am only three and a half feet high, and I have been jester to millions of sovereigns—that is, to millions of the sovereign American people, as well as to some foreign royalties.

The reason for little people taking naturally to sunshine and good-natured joking is not hard to find, for it is a simple case of Hobson's choice. It is easier to knock a man out with a joke than with a fist-blow, especially if you haven't much height and weight behind your fist. It is the better way, too, for the joke doesn't hurt. Instead of the other man's going in search of an arnica bottle or a pistol or a policeman, he generally hangs about with the hope of getting another blow of the same sort. One needn't be little to try it. Abraham Lincoln had a fist almost as big as the hand of Providence, and as long a reach as John L. Sullivan, but he always used a joke instead, so men who came to growl remained to laugh. I'm not concerned about the size of my own hand, for it has been big enough to get and keep everything that belonged to me. As to reach, as long as my jests reach their mark I shan't take the trouble to measure arms with any one.

It is a Simple Case of Hobson's Choice.

There's always something in a jest—for the man who hears it. How about the jester? Well, he is easily satisfied. Most men want the earth, so they get the bad as well as the good, but the best that the world affords is good enough for the jester, so I shan't try to break the record. It is often said that the jester swims near the top. Why shouldn't he? Isn't that where the cream is? And isn't he generous enough to leave the skimmed milk for the chaps dismal enough to prefer to swim at the bottom?

I am often moved to pride when I realize how ancient is my craft. Adam did not have a jester; but he did not need one, for he was the only man—except you and I—who married the only woman in the world. Neither did old Noah have or need one, for he had the laugh on everybody else when the floods fell and he found himself in out of the rain. But as soon as the world dried out and got full enough of people to set up kings in business, the jester appears in history, and the nations without jesters to keep kings' minds in good-working order dropped out of the procession. The only one of them that survives is Persia, where John the Jester is, as he always was, in high favor at court. When trouble is in the air he merely winks at the Shah and gets off: "Oh, Pshaw!" or some other *bon mot* old enough to be sweet; then the monarch doubles up and laughs the frown from his face, and the headsman sheathes his sword and takes a day off.

Speaking of old saws that are always welcome reminds me to protest against the unthinking persons who cry "Chestnut!" against every joke that is not newly coined. In one way it is a compliment, for the chestnut is the sweetest nut that grows; but it does not reach perfection until it has had many soakings and frosts, and has been kicked about under the dead leaves so many times that if it was anything except a chestnut it would have been lost. Good stories are like good principles: the older they are, the stronger their pull.

There is not a more popular tale in the world than that of Cinderella. It is so good that nations have almost fought for the honor of originating it. Yet a few years ago some antiquarians dug some inscribed clay tablets from the ruins of an Asiatic city that was centuries old when Noah was a boy. Some sharps at that sort of thing began to decipher them, and suddenly they came upon the story of Cinderella—her golden slipper, fairy godmother, princely lover and all. But do children say "Chestnut!" if you give them this, and then tell them the story of Cinderella? Not they!—unless you don't know how to tell it. A story is like food: it doesn't matter how familiar it is, if you know how to serve it well.

Why, the story-teller, of the same old stories, too, is as busy in Persia to-day as he was thousands of years ago, and one of the most important of his duties is the passing of the hat. You will find him on the street corners of the towns with a crowd about him. When he reaches the most interesting part of the story he will stop, like the newspaper serial with "To be continued in our next." Then he passes his fez. The listeners know well what the remainder of the story will be; but instead of "Chestnut!" he hears the melodious clink of coppers.

Not only the Shah, but many a wealthy Persian keeps a jester for the sole purpose of being made to laugh when he feels dull. Some of the antics of these chaps would not seem funny to an American—such, for instance, as going about on all fours, knocking people down and dressing in fantastic attire—but there is no accounting for tastes, as the old woman said when she kissed the cow. The Shah's jester has a great swing—he has twelve houses, and not a mortgage on one of them. He also has all the wives he wants. Who says that talent is not properly appreciated in Persia?

If you will run over to Europe you will find the Irish prototype of the Persian story-teller on the streets of Dublin and Limerick. Many a time I have seen him on the street corner telling the thrilling story of how O'Shamus was shot, or some similarly cheering tale—for fighting seems the funniest of fun to an Irishman. And just before first blood is drawn, the story-teller pauses to pass the hat, into which drop hard-earned pennies that had been saved for something else. It is the old Persian act. The manner is the same, though the coat and hat are different, so I should not be surprised to learn that the Irish are direct descendants of the ancient Persians.

The Irish Prototype of the Persian Story-Teller.

It would be easy to follow the parallel and to show how from the ancient jester was evolved the modern comedian; but of the "true-blue" jesters of to-day—the men who evolve fun from their own inner consciousness—I am compelled to quote: "There are only a few of us left." Of these "entertainers," as they are called in modern parlance, I shall let out a few of the secrets which admit them to the drawing-room of England and America to put a frosting, as it were, on proceedings that otherwise might be too sweet, perhaps too heavy. The modern jester comes to the aid of the queen of the drawing-room just as the ancient one did to the monarch of old, so he is still an honored guest at the table of royalty.

II
SUNNY MEN OF SERIOUS PRESENCE

Richard Croker.—A Good Fellow and Not Hard to Approach.—If One is Not in Politics.—Croker as a Haymaker.—Does Not Keep Opinions on Tap.—He and Chauncey Depew on New York City Politics.—Croker Bewilders a London Salesman.—His Greatest Pride.—Recorder Goff.—Not as Severe as His Acts.—Justice Tempered With Mercy.—Two Puzzling Cases.

One of the privileges of a cheerful chap without any axes to grind is that of seeing behind the mask that some men of affairs are compelled to wear. Often men whom half of the world hates and the other half fears are as companionable as a hearty boy, if they are approached by a man who doesn't want anything he shouldn't have—wants nothing but a slice of honest human nature.

Such a man is Richard Croker, for years the autocrat of Tammany Hall and still believed, by many, to have the deciding word on any question of Tammany's policy. With most men it is a serious matter, requiring much negotiation, to get a word with Mr. Croker, and they dare not expect more than a word in return.

While at Richfield Springs, a few years ago, I drove out to call on Mr. Croker at his farm. I met Mrs. Croker on the piazza and was told I would probably find her husband in the hay-field; so I went around behind the stables and found the leader of Tammany Hall in his shirt-sleeves pitching hay upon a wagon. At that time an exciting political contest was "on," and New York politicians were continually telegraphing and telephoning their supreme manager,—the only man who could untangle all the hard knots,— yet from his fields Richard Croker conducted the campaign, and with so little trouble to him that it did not keep him from making sure of his hay-crop, by putting it in himself.

In later years I saw much more of Mr. Croker, for I was often his guest at Wantage, his country home in England, and I could not help studying him closely, for he was a most interesting man. In appearance he suggested General Grant; he was of Grant's stature and build, his close-cropped beard and quiet but observant eyes recalled Grant, and his face, like the great general's, suggested bulldog courage and tenacity, as well as the high sense of self-reliance that makes a man the leader of his fellow men. Few of his closest associates know more of him than his face expresses, for he is possessed of and by the rarest of all human qualities—that of keeping his opinions to himself. Most political leaders say things which bob up later to torment them, but Croker's political enemies never have the luck of giving him his own words to eat. He can and does talk freely with men whom he likes and who are not tale-bearers, but he never talks from the judgment seat. Even about ordinary affairs he is too modest and sensible to play Sir Oracle. One day he chanced to be off his guard and gave me a positive opinion on a certain subject; when afterward I recalled it to him he exclaimed: "Marshall, did I tell you that?" It amazed him that he had expressed an opinion.

During one of my visits to Wantage Mr. Croker and I were together almost continually for a week; he not only survived it, but was a most attentive and companionable host. His son Bert was fond of getting up early in the morning to hunt mushrooms, and in order to be awakened he would set an alarm clock. "Early morning" in England and at that season of the year was from three to four o'clock, for dawn comes much earlier than with us. His father did not wish him to arise so early, so he would go softly into Bert's room and turn off the alarm, to assure a full night sleep for the boy. The fact that he could not hear the alarm worried Bert so greatly that he placed the clock directly over his head, hanging it to a string from the ceiling. But even in this position Mr. Croker succeeded in manipulating it, and he gleefully told me of it at the time.

One day, in London, Mr. Croker called for me and took me to see Mr. Depew, who had recently arrived. We drove to the Savoy and found Mr. Depew on the steps, just starting for Paris. He exclaimed:

"Hello? What are you two fellows doing together?—fixing up the election?"

This was just before Van Wyck was elected mayor; Mr. Strong's enforcement of the liquor law had been so vigorous as to enrage many bibulous voters. As he bade us good-bye Mr. Depew found time to say to Mr. Croker,

"All your party will have to do will be to hold their hats and catch the votes."

At the time of the Queen's Jubilee we were invited to view the procession from Mr. Jefferson Levy's apartment in Piccadilly, but Mr. Croker declined; he told me afterward that he would have offended many Irish voters in America had he appeared in any way to honor the Queen.

Before starting from London for Wantage one day, Mr. Croker asked me to go to a furniture dealer's with him; he had some purchases to make. As we entered the place he said to me, "We've only half an hour in which to catch the train"—but the way he bought furniture did not make him lose the train. He would say, pointing to a dresser,

"How much is that?"

"Six guineas, sir."

"Give me six of them."

Pointing to another,

"How much is that one?"

"Five guineas, sir."

"Well, seven of those"—and so on.

With such rapid fire, even though he expended more than a thousand dollars, and not at haphazard either, there was ample time to catch the train. The incident, though slight in itself, is indicative of his quickness of decision; but it so utterly upset the dealers, accustomed to English deliberation, that he begged permission to wait until next day to prepare an itemized bill.

Mr. Croker's quiet unobtrusive manner, which has so often deceived his political enemies into believing that he was doing nothing, dates back a great many years—as far back as his courtship. The future Mrs. Croker and her sister were charming girls and their home was the social rendezvous of all young people of the vicinity. Their father was a jolly good fellow and as popular as his daughters; when the latter went to a dance he was always their chaperon, and a most discreet one he was for he always went up-stairs and slept until the time to go home. Mr. Croker was at the house a great deal but was so quiet and devoted so much time to chat with the father that no one suspected that one of the daughters was the real attraction, but with the quiet persistence that had always characterized him he "won out."

Great soldiers delight in fighting their battles o'er and no one begrudges them the pleasure. Mr. Croker has been in some desperate fights and won some great victories. Hoping for a story or more about them I one day asked him of what in his life he was most proud. His reply indicated the key-note of his nature, for it was:

"That I have never gone back on my word."

Another man who has kept many thousands of smart fellows uncomfortably awake and in fear is Recorder Goff. When he conducted the inquiries of the Lexow Committee he extracted so much startling testimony from men whom no one believed could be made to confess anything, that a lot of fairly discreet citizens were almost afraid to look him in the eye, for fear he would ferret out all their private affairs. I had never seen him, but I had mentally made a distinct picture of him as a tall, thin, dark-browed, austere, cold character, rather on the order of a Grand Inquisitor, as generally accepted. When we met it was at a dinner, where I sat beside him and had to retouch almost every detail of my picture, for, although tall and thin, he was blonde and rosy, of sanguine temperament, with merry eyes, a genial smile and as talkative as every good fellow ought to be.

The acquaintance begun at that dinner-table was continued most pleasantly by many meetings in Central Park, which both of us frequented on our bicycles. One day, while we were resting in the shadow of Daniel Webster's statue, I made bold to ask him how he came by his marvelous power of extracting the truth from unwilling occupants of the witness-box. He murmured something self-deprecatory, but told me the following story in illustration of one of his indirect methods and also of how truth will persist in muddling the wits of a liar.

"A man was brought before me accused of killing another man with a bottle. He had a friend whose mother was on the witness stand and she tried to save her son's friend, though she perjured herself to do so. She swore she had seen the murderer and could describe him. I was convinced of the accused's guilt and the woman's perjury, and I determined to surprise her into confession.

"I got seven men of varying appearance who were in the court-room to stand up, which they did, though greatly mystified, for they were present only as spectators. I asked the woman if the first man was the murderer. She promptly answered 'No,' to his great relief.

"'But,' I said, 'he resembles the murderer, doesn't he? He is the same height?'

"'Oh, no,' she answered, 'he is much taller.' Motioning the first man to sit down, I pointed to No. 2, and asked:

"'This man is the same height as the murderer, is he not?'

"'Yes, exactly.' I asked the man his height, and he said 'five feet seven.' He was told to sit down, and No. 3, who had a head of most uncompromising red hair, was brought forward.

"'You said the murderer had red hair like this man, didn't you?'

"'Oh, no—brown, curly hair.'

"'Were his eyes like this man's?'

"'No, they were brown.'

"Number four, who had fine teeth, was asked to open his mouth, greatly to his embarrassment.

"'Were the murderer's teeth like this man's?'

"'No, he had two gold teeth, one on each side.'

"Number five was rather stout and the woman thought the murderer about his size; he weighed one hundred and sixty. Six and seven were looked at and sent back to their seats, nervous and perspiring. Then I said:

"'We find from this woman's testimony that the murderer was about five feet seven in height, weighed one hundred and sixty, had dark curly hair, brown eyes, two gold teeth and a habit of keeping his hands in his pockets.'

"By this time the prisoner was white and shaking, for bit by bit the witness had described him exactly. When the woman realized what she had done she broke down and confessed that the prisoner was the real criminal."

It was charged that a man brought before Recorder Goff for theft was an old offender and had served a term in states prison, but the accused denied it and no amount of cross-questioning by the prosecution could shake his denial. Mr. Goff noticed that he had lost a thumb; as prisoners are generally given a name by their comrades, signifying some physical peculiarity, the Recorder said:

"While in prison you were known as One-Thumbed Jack." Taken off his guard, the man asked:

"How did you know that?"

"Then you are an ex-convict?"

"Well, yes, sir, but I had honest reasons for not wanting it known and I'd like to speak to you alone, sir."

Mr. Goff granted the request and they retired to a small room where the prisoner after telling his real name, related a touching story of devotion to a young sister whom he brought up and educated with the proceeds of his earlier crimes. While serving his prison term he had written her letters which his pals posted for him in different parts of the world to make her believe he was traveling so constantly that any letters from her could not reach him. This sister was now married and had two children and it would break her heart to find out that her brother was a convict or had ever been one. So he wished to be sentenced under another name. Mr. Goff said:

"I will suspend sentence."

Later the man's statements were investigated and found to be true. So his request to be sentenced under an assumed name was granted. Farther, he got but two years, although he would have been "sent up" for ten years had it not been for his story—a fact which shows how in Recorder Goff, the city's greatest terror to evil-doers, justice is tempered with mercy.

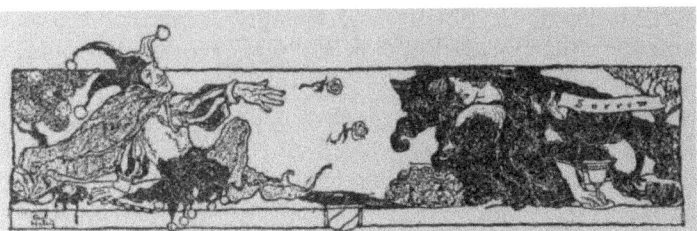

III
AT THE WHITE HOUSE AND NEAR IT

My Prophecy to "Major" McKinley.—President McKinley Becomes "One of the Boys" of My Audience; His Attention to His Wife.—How He Won a Vermont City.—A Story of the Spanish War.—My First Meeting With President Harrison.—A Second and More Pleasing One.—A Chance Which I Gladly Lost.—Some of President Harrison's Stories.—I Led a Parade Given in His Honor.—Vice-Presidents Morton and Hobart.

It had been my good fortune to meet several presidents of the United States, as well as some gentlemen who would have occupied the White House had the president died, and I learned that, in spite of their many torments and tormentors, they all liked to get into the sunshine and that they had done it so much that the sunshine had returned the compliment right heartily, as is its way "in such case made and provided."

Some years ago while entering a New York hotel to call on Madame Patti I chanced to meet in the corridor William McKinley, who was then governor of Ohio, though his New York acquaintances still called him "Major." His was one of the big, broad natures that put all of a man's character in full view, and there was a great lot in McKinley's face that day,—thoughtfulness, self-reliance, strength, honesty, as well as some qualities that seldom combine in one man—simplicity and shrewdness, modesty and boldness, serious purpose and cheerfulness, that I became quite happy in contemplation of him as a trusty all-around American. He greeted me very cordially and as I was smiling broadly, he asked:

"What pleases you, Marshall?"

"The fact that I am shaking hands with the future president of the United States," I replied.

Some years afterward, when Mr. McKinley had fulfilled my prophecy, I was the guest of D. A. Loring, at Lake Champlain, and the president and most of his cabinet were at the same hotel. Besides Mr. and Mrs. McKinley there were Vice-President and Mrs. Hobart, Secretary of War Alger and Mrs. Alger, Postmaster General Geary and Mrs. Geary, Cornelius N. Bliss, Secretary of the Interior, and others. Every one at the hotel treated the distinguished guest with the greatest consideration, by letting him entirely alone, so that he got the rest he sorely needed. He walked much about the grounds, enjoying the bracing atmosphere and peaceful, beautiful surroundings.

One day I went into the bowling alley to spend half an hour or more with the boys who set up the pins; boys are always my friends, and I was going to do some card and sleight-of-hand tricks for these little fellows. Just as I had gathered them about me and started to amuse them, Mr. McKinley came to the door and looked in, smiled, came over to us and asked what was going on. I replied:

"Well, Mr. President, I was just doing some tricks to amuse the boys."

"Then I'm one of the boys," said the president of the United States. He sat down in the circle and was one of my most attentive auditors. When I had finished he walked apart with me and said:

"Marshall, do you remember meeting me in the Windsor Hotel, New York, and saying you were shaking hands with the future president of the United States?"

"I recall it very distinctly," I replied.

"I have just been thinking," he said, "of that—to me, strange prophecy. You must be possessed of some clairvoyant power." There are some things you can't tell a man to his face, so I didn't explain to him that a man with a character like his couldn't help becoming president, when the whole country had come to know him.

I shall never forget what I saw of his lover-like devotion to his invalid wife, nor her evident gratitude for his every service, nor the sweet solicitude and pride with which she regarded him. One day his brother Abner arrived, went to the portion of the hotel reserved for the president, met Mrs. McKinley and asked:

"Is William in?"

"Yes," was the reply, "but I shall not let you see him for an hour. He is resting."

A little incident that was described to me by an eye-witness brought out one of the qualities which endeared President McKinley to his fellow countrymen. While on a brief visit across the lake, in Vermont, he was driving through a small city, followed by a great procession of people who had turned out in his honor. While passing through the main street he noticed an old man seated on the piazza of a modest dwelling, and asked the mayor, who was beside him in the carriage,

"Who is that old gentleman?"

"That is Mr. Philip, father of Captain Philip, of the battleship *Texas*," was the reply.

"I thought that must be he," said the president. "Will you kindly stop the carriage?"

The carriage stopped and so did the mile or more of procession, while the president jumped out, unassisted, ran up the steps, grasped the hand of the astonished and delighted old man, and said:

"Mr. Philip, I want to congratulate you on having such a son as Captain Philip, and I feel that the thanks of the nation are due you for having given the world such a brave, patriotic man."

The old man, tremulous with gratification, could scarcely find words with which to thank the head of the nation for his appreciative attention, but the president's simple, friendly manner quickly put him at his ease and the two men chatted freely for several minutes, the president evidently enjoying it keenly. Then after a hearty invitation to visit him at the White House, Mr. McKinley got into his carriage and the procession again started.

Mention of the *Texas* recalls a visit I made to her when she was at the New York Navy Yard for repairs, after the fight with Cervera's fleet, in which the *Texas* was the principal American sufferer. A young officer took me about the ship, showed me her honorable wounds, repeated Captain Philip's historic remark, made after the battle,—"Don't cheer, boys; the poor fellows are dying," and told me the following story:

One of our Irish sailors was very active in saving the Spaniards in the water, throwing them ropes, boxes and everything floatable he could find. But there was one Spaniard who missed everything that was thrown him. Just before the battle we had had religious service and the altar was still on deck, so our Irishman grabbed it, heaved it overboard and yelled:

"There, ye haythen! If *that* won't save ye, nothin' ever will."

While Mr. Harrison was president I became pleasantly acquainted with his son Russell, who, having read of President Cleveland's very kind treatment of me when I went to him with a letter of introduction from Henry Ward Beecher, wanted me to meet his father and gave me a letter to that effect. My visit to the White House was quite impressive—to me. Soon after I reached Chamberlain's, at Washington, a messenger arrived and informed me that the President had received my letter of introduction and desired me to call the next morning at ten o'clock, which I did.

After passing the sentinels at the door I was taken into the room of Mr. Private Secretary "Lije" Halford, who greeted me cordially and said: "Mr. Wilder, the president will see you." I was ushered into Mr. Harrison's presence, and the following conversation ensued:

"Mr. President, this is Mr. Wilder."

"How do you do, Mr. Wilder?"

"How do you do, Mr. President?"

A profound silence followed; it seemed to me to be several minutes long; then I said:

"Good-day, Mr. President."

"Good-day, Mr. Wilder."

After leaving the room I turned to Mr. Halford, raised my coat-tails and asked:

"Won't you please kick me?"

Of course I had to refer to the incident in my monologue that season, for it isn't every day that a professional entertainer is invited to call at the White House. But I did not care to tell exactly what occurred, so I adopted an old minstrel joke and said:

"I called on the president the other day. I walked in, in a familiar way, and said, 'How do you do, Mr. President?' He said, 'Sir, I cannot place you.' 'Well,' I replied, 'that's what I'm here for.'"

I afterward heard that President Harrison was very cold and lacked cordiality; still later I discovered, with my own eyes and ears, that he had a kind heart and genial nature. One summer while I was at Saratoga I was asked by Mr. W. J. Arkell to Mount McGregor, to meet President Harrison at dinner and to become a member of a fishing party. The occasion was the president's birthday, and the invitation was the more welcome when I learned that a list of the people at the Saratoga hotels had been shown the president, who had himself selected the guests for his birthday celebration. At Mount McGregor I found, as one always finds, wherever the President of the United States is staying a few days, thirty or forty newspaper correspondents, all of whom I knew and most of whom professed to doubt my ability to make the president laugh. This did not worry me, for I don't love trouble enough to look ahead for it, and dinner time, when the laughing was to begin, was a few hours distant.

We all went by carriage to a stream about five miles away and all helped fill the president's basket with fish,—for which he got full credit, in the next day's newspapers. My own contributions were few and small, for I never was a good fisherman. So I was grateful when Russell Harrison took me to a little pool where he was sure we would have great luck. But not a bite did either of us get. Then I recalled something that a veteran fisherman played on me when I was too young to be suspicious; it was to beat the water to attract the attention of the fish. Russell kindly assisted me at beating the water, but the fish beat us both by keeping away.

When we got back to the hotel and to the banquet it was announced that there were to be no speeches, but the president would make a few remarks and I would be called on for a few stories. Consequently I had no mind or appetite for dinner, for most of the guests were newspaper men who had been surfeited with stories ever since they entered the business, and the most important listener would be the president, who the boys had said I couldn't make laugh.

I was still mentally searching my repertoire, although I had already selected a lot of richness, when the president arose and made some general remarks. But it was impossible for him to forget that at this same place—Mount McGregor, Ex-President Grant breathed his last, so Mr. Harrison's concluding remarks were on the line that any other whole-hearted American would have struck in similar circumstances. As I am a whole-hearted American myself, they struck me just where I live, and I am not ashamed to confess that they knocked me out.

So, when I was called upon, I declined to respond. Several friends came to my chair and whispered: "Go ahead, Marsh." "Don't lose the chance of your life; don't you know whatever is said at this dinner will be telegraphed all over the United States?" But I held my tongue—or it held itself. There is a place for every thing; a table at which the President of the United States had just been talking most feelingly of the pathetic passing of another president was no place for a joke—much less for a budget of jokes, so instead of making the president laugh I allowed the newspaper men to have the laugh on me. In the circumstances they were welcome to it.

"I allowed the newspaper men to have a laugh on me."

Nevertheless I succeeded, for the president succeeded in breaking the strain upon him, and later in the day at his own cottage he transfixed me with a merry twinkle of his eye and said:

"Marshall, what's this story you've been telling about your visit to the White House?"

I saw I was in for it, so I repeated the minstrel joke, already recorded. He laughed so heartily that there wasn't enough unbroken ice between us to hold up a dancing mosquito, so I made bold to tell him that some men insisted that he did not appreciate humor. Then he laughed again; I wish I could have photographed that laugh, for there was enough worldly wisdom in it to lessen the number of cranks and office seekers at the White House for years to come. But I hadn't much time to think about it, for we began swapping yarns and kept at it so long that I suddenly reminded myself, with a sense of guilt, that I was robbing the ruler of the greatest nation on earth of some of his invaluable time. Never mind about my own stories that evening, but here is one that President Harrison told me, to illustrate the skill of some men in talking their way out of a tight place.

There was a man in Indiana who had a way of taking his own advice, though he generally had to do things afterward to get even with himself. He was a hog dealer, and one season he drove a lot of hogs to Indianapolis, about a hundred miles distant, though he could get nearly as good a price at a town much nearer home. Arrived at Indianapolis, he learned that prices had gone down, so he held on for a rise, but when offered a good price he stood out for more, and insisted that if he did not get it he would drive the hogs back home, which he finally did, and sold them for less than was offered him in the city. When one of his friends asked him why he had acted so unwisely he replied:

"I wanted to get even with them city hog-buyers."

"But did you?"

"Well, they didn't get my hogs."

"But what did you get out of the transaction?"

"Get? Why, bless your thick skull, I got the society of the hogs all the way back home."

I had long been puzzled as to the origin of the word "jay," as applied to "easy marks" among countrymen, and I told the president so. He modestly admitted that I had come to the right shop for information; then he told me this story:

"Winter was coming on and a blue jay made up his mind that he would prepare for it. He found a vacant hut with a knot-hole in the roof, and he said to himself, 'Here's a good place to store my winter supplies,' so he began to collect provender. His acquaintances who passed by saw what he was doing; then they laughed and took a rest, for they knew how to get in by the side door. Whenever he dropped a nut or a bit of meat through the knot-hole they would hop in below and gobble it. So, Marshall, next time you hear any one called a 'jay' I'm sure you'll know what it means."

The next morning, when we all met on the president's special train en route to Saratoga, my newspaper friends twitted me anew on not having made the president laugh, but I said: "Now, boys, you wait." Then I was so impudent as to approach the president and say:

"Mr. President, I am very glad to have had you with me on this fishing trip, and I hope whenever you want to go off on a similar affair you will let me know it. At the foot of the mountain a band of music and escort of troops are waiting for me, and in the hurry I may not be able to say good-bye to you, so I say it now." But not one eyelash of the president quivered as he shook hands with me and replied: "Glad to have met you, Mr. Wilder," so the newspaper boys certainly did have the laugh on me.

But the day was still young. Arrived at the Saratoga depot, all hurried into carriages. Waiting until all were seated and started in procession, I found an open landau and gave the driver the name of my hotel. "All right, Mr. Wilder," was the reply, which did not startle me, for I am pretty well known in Saratoga by the cabbies—and the police. I said:

"Make a short cut, get out of the crowd and get me to the hotel as soon as possible, so I may avoid the parade." He endeavored to get out, but he got in; and in trying to extricate himself he succeeded in driving through the band and past the troops and finally beside the carriages of the president and his guests. I took advantage of the occasion; as I passed the president I stood up (though it made little difference whether I sat or stood, for not much of me was visible over the top of the carriage door) and I bowed my prettiest. The president raised his hat, as did the other guests, and I led that procession down Saratoga's Broadway, the sidewalks of which were crowded with New York and Brooklyn people who knew me and to whom I bowed, right and left, to the end of the route, where one of the newspaper men said:

"Marsh usually gets there."

In Mr. McKinley's first term I fell in conversation at a hotel with a gentleman of manner so genial that I never forgot him. We exchanged a lot of stories, at which I got more than I gave, but suddenly the gentleman said:

"I can see, Mr. Wilder, that you don't recognize me."

"Well, really, I don't," I replied, with an apologetic laugh. "You must pardon me; I meet so many. May I ask your name?"

"Certainly. It is Garret A. Hobart."

"The Vice-president of the United States! Well, that isn't anything against you"—for I had to say something, to keep from collapsing. He seemed greatly amused, and I could not help wondering if in any other country of the world a high official of the government could be picked up in a hotel corridor, be chatted with, then be compelled to introduce himself, and throughout all conduct himself as if he were no one in particular.

Levi P. Morton, ex-vice-president, has been out of politics for some years, yet he is remembered as a man who could tell good stories to illustrate his points. Here is one of them:

"The General doubled on his tracks."

"Not far from my country place is a farmer noted for his fine, large cattle. People come from everywhere to look at his Durhams and Alderneys, but they have to be careful how they venture into the pastures, for some of the bulls are ferocious. A certain major-general, who was very proud of his title, was visiting near by, and one day while walking he cut across the fields to shorten distance. Before he knew of his danger a big bull, bellowing and with tossing head, began to chase him. The general was a swift runner, and made good time, but the animal too was lively, so when the general reached a fence he dared not stop to climb for the bull was near enough to—well, help him. The general doubled on his tracks several times, but the bull kept dangerously near. Suddenly a gate offered a chance to shut off pursuit. Near the gate stood the farmer, who had been viewing the chase; the panting general turned on him fiercely and asked, between gasps:

"'Sir—sir—did you—see your bull chasing—me?'

"'Ya-as,' drawled the farmer.

"'Is that all you have to say, sir? Do you know whom that bull was chasing?'

"'You, I guess.'

"'But do you know who I am, sir? I am General Blank.'"

"'Wa-all, why didn't you tell that to the bull?'"

IV
STORY-TELLING AS AN ART

Different Ways of Story-telling.—The Slow Story-teller.—Lincoln's Stories.—Bad Telling of Good Stories.—The Right Way to Tell a Story.—The Humorous, the Comic and the Witty Story.—Artemus Ward, Robert J. Burdette and Mark Twain as Story-tellers.

The ways of story-tellers differ almost as widely and strangely as the ways of politicians—or women—yet every man's way is the best and only one to him. I know men who consume so much time in unloading a story that they remind me of a ship-captain who had just taken a pilot and was anxious to get into port. The pilot knew all the channels and shoals of the vicinity, and being a cautious old chap he wasn't going to take any risks, so he backed and filled and crisscrossed so many times that the captain growled: "Hang him! He needs the Whole Atlantic Ocean to turn around in."

Yet a lot of these long-winded story-tellers "get there"—and they deserve to, not only because a hearty laugh follows, but because hard work deserves its reward. As to that, Abraham Lincoln, long before he became president, and when time was of no consequence, had some stories almost as long as old-fashioned sermons; but nobody left his seat by the stove at the country store, or his leaning place at the post-office, or his chair on the hotel piazza until "Abe" had reached the point. But there never was more than one Abraham Lincoln. To-day a long-winded story-teller can disperse a crowd about as quickly as a man with a bad case of smallpox.

But it isn't always length that troubles the listener—the way in which a tale is told is the thing, whether the tale itself be good or bad. It is never safe for some people to repeat a good story they have heard, for they may tell it in a fashion that is like being bitten to death by a duck.

I do not claim originality for my own method and material. I simply tell a story, using whatever material comes my way. Often a friend will tell me of something he has seen or heard; I will reconstruct his narrative, without tampering with the facts, yet so that the people of whom he told it will not recognize it.

There is nothing, except advice, of which the world is more generous than stories. Everybody tells them. They mean well; they want to make you laugh, and they deserve credit for their intention. Yet when neighbor Smith or Brown calls you aside, looks as if he was almost bursting with something good, and then gets off a yarn that was funny when he heard it, but in which you can't discern the ghost of a laugh—why, you can't help wondering whether Smith's or Brown's funny-bone hasn't dropped off somewhere, without its owner's knowledge; you also can't help wishing that he may find it before he buttonholes you again.

It seems to me that the supreme art of telling a story is to tell it quickly and hide the nub so that the hearer's wits must find it. But it is possible for some people to tell it quickly at the expense of the essential parts, either through forgetfulness or by not knowing them at sight. For example, here is a tale I heard not long ago:

"The other night Ezra Kendall told about an Irishman who had a habit of walking in a graveyard about twelve o'clock at night. Some boys of the neighborhood planned to so dig and conceal a grave that the Irishman would fall into it; another man was to drape himself in a sheet, to scare Mike. The night arrived, the Irishman took his customary walk and fell into the hole prepared for him. A boy in a white sheet arose, and said in a sepulchral voice:

"'What are you doing in my grave?'

"'What are you doin' out of it?' Mike replied."

Soon afterward an amateur gave me the story as follows:

"I heard a story the other day by a man named Kendall about a man who went out in a graveyard at night to walk, about twelve o'clock. He fell into a ditch, and another fellow happened along and said, 'What are you doing out of it?'—or something like that. I know I laughed like the deuce when I heard it."

"What are you doing in my grave?"

But even when a story has been committed to memory or written in shorthand on a shirt-cuff, to be read off without a word lost or misplaced, much depends upon the teller. Some people's voices are so effective that they can tell a story in the dark and "make good"; others can't get through without calling all their features to help, with some assistance from their arms and legs. One man will lead you with his eye alone to the point of a story; another will drawl and stammer as if he had nothing to say, yet startle you into a laugh a minute.

Of course a great deal depends on the story itself. People are too grateful for a laugh to look backward and analyze the story that compelled it; they generally believe that fun is fun, and that is about as much as any one knows of it. The truth is that while there are all kinds of stories there is only one kind of humor.

As a rule, humorous stories are of American origin, comic stories are English, and witty stories are French. The humorous story depends upon the incidents and the manner of telling; comic and witty stories depend upon the matter. The humorous story may be spun out to any length; it may wander about as it pleases, and arrive at nowhere in particular; but the comic or witty story must be brief, and end in a sharp point. The humorous story bubbles along continually; the other kinds burst. The humorous tale is entirely a work of art, and only an artist can tell it; while the witty or comic story—oh, any one who knows it can tell it.

The act of telling a humorous story—by word of mouth, understand, not in print—was created in America, and has remained at home, in spite of many earnest endeavors to domesticate it abroad, and even to counterfeit it. It is generally told gravely, the teller doing his best to disguise his attempt to inflict anything funny on his listeners; but the man with a comic story generally tells you beforehand that it is one of the funniest things he ever heard, and he is the first one to laugh—when he reaches the end.

One of the dreadfulest inflictions that suffering humanity ever endures is the result of amateur efforts to transform the humorous into the comic, or *vice versa*. It reminds one of Frank Stockton's tearful tale of what came of one of the best things in Pickwick by being translated into classical Greek and then brought back into English.

The Rev. Robert J. Burdette, who used to write columns of capital humor for *The Burlington Hawkeye* and told scores of stories superbly, made his first visit to New York about twenty years ago, and was at once spirited to a notable club where he told stories leisurely until half the hearers ached with laughter and the other half were threatened with apoplexy. Every one present declared it the red letter night of the club, and members who had missed it came around and demanded the stories at second-hand. Some efforts were made to oblige them, but without avail, for the tellers had twisted their recollections of the stories into comic jokes; so they hunted the town for Burdette to help them out of their muddle.

The late Artemus Ward, who a generation ago carried a tidal wave of humor from Maine to California, with some generous overflows each side of its course, had a long serious face and a drawling voice; so when he lectured in churches, as he frequently did, a late-comer might have mistaken him for a minister, though not for very long. He would drawl along without giving the slightest indication of what was coming. When the joke was unloaded and the audience got hold of it he would look up with seemingly innocent wonder as to what people were laughing at. This expression of his countenance always brought another laugh. He could get laughs out of nothing, by mixing the absurd and the unexpected, and then backing the combination with a solemn face and earnest manner. For instance, it was worth a ten-mile walk after dark on a corduroy road to hear him say: "I once knew a man in New Zealand who hadn't a tooth in his head"—here he would pause for some time, look reminiscent, and continue, "And yet he could beat a base-drum better than any other man I ever knew."

Mark Twain is another famous humorist who can use a serious countenance and hesitating voice with wonderful effect in a story. His tale of "The Golden Arm" was the best thing of its kind I ever heard—when told as he himself told it—but everything depended on suddenness and unexpectedness of climax. Here it is, as he gave it:—

"Once 'pon a time dey wuz a mons'us mean man, en' he live 'way out in de prairie all 'lone by himself, 'cep'n he had a wife. En' bimeby she died, en' he took en' toted her 'way out da' in de prairie en' buried her. Well, she had a golden arm all solid gold, f'om de shoulder down. He wuz pow'ful mean—pow'ful; en' dat night he couldn't sleep, 'coze he wanted dat golden arm so bad.

"When it come midnight he couldn't stan' it no mo', so he got up, he did, en' tuk his lantern en' shoved out troo de storm en' dug her up en' got de golden arm; en' he bent his head down 'gin de wind, en' plowed en' plowed en' plowed troo de snow. Den all on a sudden he stop" (make a considerable pause here, and look startled, and take a listening attitude) "en' say:

"My lan', what's dat? En' he listen, en' listen, en' de wind say" (set your teeth together, and imitate the wailing and wheezing sing-song of the wind): "'Buzz-z-zzz!' en' den, way back yonder whah de grave is, he hear a voice—he hear a voice all mix up in de win'—can't hardly tell 'em 'part: 'Bzzz-zzz—w-h-o—g-o-t—m-y g-o-l-d-e-n arm?'" (You must begin to shiver violently now.)

"She'll fetch a dear little yelp—"

"En' he begin to shiver en' shake, en' say: 'Oh, my! Oh, my lan'!' En' de win' blow de lantern out, en' de snow en' de sleet blow in his face en' 'most choke him, en' he start a-plowin' knee-deep toward home, mos' dead, he so sk'yeerd, en' pooty soon he hear de voice again, en'" (pause) "it 'us comin' after him: 'Buzzz-zzz—w-h-o—g-o-t m-y g-o-l-d-e-n—arm?'

"When he git to de pasture he hear it agin—closter, now, en' a comin' back dab in de dark en' de storm" (repeat the wind and the voice). "When he git to de house he rush up-stairs, en' jump in de bed, en' kiver up head en' years, en' lay dah a-shiverin' en' a-shakin', en' den 'way out dah he hear it agin, en' a-comin'! En' bimeby he hear" (pause—awed; listening attitude) "—at—pat—pat—pat—hit's a-comin' up-stairs! Den he hear de latch, en' he knows it's in de room.

"Den pooty soon he knows it's—standin' by de bed!" (Pause.) "Den he knows it's a-bendin' down over him,—en' he cain't sca'cely git his breaf! Den—den he seem to feel somethin' c-o-l-d, right down neah agin' his head!" (Pause.)

"Den de voice say, right at his year: 'W-h-o g-o-t m-y g-o-l-d-e-n arm?'" You must wail it out plaintively and accusingly; then you stare steadily and impressively into the face of the farthest-gone auditor—a girl, preferably—and let that awe-inspiring pause begin to build itself in the deep hush. When it has reached exactly the right length, jump suddenly toward that girl and yell: "'*You've* got it!'"

If you have got the pause right, she'll fetch a dear little yelp and spring right out of her shoes; but you must get the pause right, and you will find it the most troublesome and aggravating and uncertain thing you ever undertook.

V
ACTORS' JOKES

All of Them Full of Humor at All Times.—"Joe" Jefferson.—J. K. Emmett.—Fay Templeton.—Willie Collier.—An Actor's Portrait on a Church Wall.—"Gus" Thomas, the Playwright.—Stuart Robson.—Henry Dixey.—Evans and Hoey.—Charles Hoyt.—Wilson Barrett.—W. S. Gilbert.—Henry Irving.

Actors are the most incessant jokers alive. Whether rich or poor, obscure or prominent, drunk or sober, prosperous or not knowing where the next meal is to come from, or whether there will be any next meal, they have always something funny at the tips of their tongues, and managers and dramatic authors as a rule are full of humorous explosives that clear the dull air and let in the sunshine. They are masters at repartee, yet as willing to turn a joke on themselves as on one another, and they can work a pun most brilliantly.

Joseph Jefferson one day called on President Cleveland with General Sherman, and carried a small package with him. All his friends know that dear old "Joe" is forgetful, so when the visitors were going the general called attention to the package and asked: "Jefferson, isn't this yours?"

"Great Cæsar, Sherman," Jefferson replied, "you have saved my life!" The "life" referred to was the manuscript of his then uncompleted biography. Jefferson delights in telling of a new playmate of one of his sons, who asked another boy who young Jefferson was, and was told:

"Oh, his father works in a theatre somewhere."

"Pete" Dailey, while enjoying a short vacation, visited a New York theatre when business was dull. Being asked afterward how large the audience was, he replied: "I could lick all three of them."

On meeting a friend who was "fleshing up," he exclaimed: "You are getting so stout that I thought some one was with you."

J. K. Emmett tells of a heathenish old farmer and his wife who strayed into a church and heard the minister say: "Jesus died for sinners." The old man nudged his wife, and whispered:

"Serves us right for not knowin' it, Marthey. We hain't took a newspaper in thirty year."

Fay Templeton tells of a colored girl, whose mother shouted: "Mandy, your heel's on fire!" and the girl replied: "Which one, mother?" The girl was so untruthful that her discouraged mother said: "When you die, dey's going to say: 'Here lies Mandy Hopkins, and de trufe never came out of her when she was alive.'"

"Actors are the Most Incessant Jokers Alive."

I have been the subject of some actors' jokes, and enjoyed the fun as much as any one. May Irwin had two sons, who early in life were susceptible to the seductive cigarette, against which she cautioned them earnestly. I entered a restaurant one day where she and her sons were dining, and she called me over and gave me an opportunity to become acquainted with the little fellows. After I left them, one turned to his mother and asked:

"What makes that little man so short?"

"Smoking cigarettes," she replied. And they never smoked again.

He Smokes Cigarettes.

Willie Collier invited me one summer to his beautiful home at St. James, Long Island. He was out when I arrived, and when he returned, Mrs. Collier said to him:

"You're going to have Marshall P. Wilder for dinner," and Willie replied:

"I'd rather have lamb."

There is a colony of theatrical people near Collier, and they have a small theatre in which a dazzling array of talent sometimes appears, although the performances are impromptu affairs. On Sundays this theatre serves as a church for the Catholics of the vicinity. At one side hangs a large lithograph of Willie Collier, concerning which the following conversation between the two Irishmen was overheard:

"I wint into the church this mornin' airly, while it was pretty dark, an' I see a picture hanging there, an' thinkin' it must be one av the saints I wint down on me knees an' said me prayers before it. When I opened me eyes they'd got used to the dark, an' if I didn't see it was a picture av that actor-man beyant that they call Willie Collier!"

"An' what did' you do?" asked the other Irishman.

"Sure, I tuk' back as much av me prayers as I cud."

Augustus Thomas, the playwright, who is always "Gus" except on the back of an envelop or the bottom of his own check, was chairman of a Lambs' Club dinner at which I was to speak. When I began, he joked me on my shortness by saying:

"Mr. Wilder will please rise when making a speech."

I was able to retort by saying: "I will; but you won't believe it."

When an acquaintance said to him after being wearied by a play: "That was the slowest performance I ever saw. Strange, too, for it had a run of a hundred nights in London!" Thomas replied:

"That's the trouble. It's exhausted its speed."

He was standing behind the scenes one night with Miss Georgia Busbey, who while waiting for her cue, said: "Tell me a story, Mr. Thomas, before I go on."

"It must be a quick witty one then, Miss Busbey."

"I know it, but I've come to the right place for it."

Stuart Robson was present at a Lambs' Club dinner of which Mr. Thomas was chairman; but he endeavored to hide when called on for a speech. Thousands of successful appearances on the stage never cured him of his constitutional bashfulness.

Thomas said: "Is Mr. Robson here? If he has not gone, we should like to hear from him."

Robson said: "Mr. Thomas, will you kindly consider that I have gone?"

Thomas replied: "While the drama lasts, Mr. Robson can never go."

Robson had been a close neighbor and friend for many years to Lawrence Barrett. His bosom friend Marshall Lewis fell in love with Barrett's charming daughter Millie, and Robson pretended to think it was the greatest joke in the world.

"Why don't you go in, and win and marry her, Marshall?" he used to say in the squeaky voice which was not for the stage alone. "I'll tell you what I'll do—the day you marry Millie Barrett I'll give you five thousand dollars."

This went on for some time, until to Robson's astonishment and chagrin Miss Barrett accepted Lewis.

By the way, when Barrett learned of it he exclaimed: "My dear boy, you don't know what you're doing. You are robbing me out of my only remaining daughter."

"Not at all," Lewis replied, with a slap on the back of his father-in-law elect. "I'm merely giving you another son."

When the marriage day came Robson did not attend the ceremony; but he sent his daughter Alicia in his place, and gave her a check for five thousand dollars, drawn to Lewis' order, but with emphatic orders not to part from it until Lewis and Miss Barrett were pronounced man and wife. When Alicia returned her father asked her if she had given Lewis the check.

The girl replied: "Yes, father."

"What did he do and say?" Robson inquired impatiently.

"Why, father, he was so overcome that he cried for a minute after I gave it to him."

"Egad!" squeaked Robson, "was that all? Why, I cried for an hour when I wrote it."

Henry Dixey is an adept at the leisurely tale, which is a word picture from start to finish. Here is a sample:

In one of the country stores, where they sell everything from a silk dress and a tub of butter to a hot drink and a cold meal, a lot of farmers were sitting around the stove one cold winter day, when in came Farmer Evans, who was greeted with:

"How d'do, Ezry?"

"How d'do boys?" After awhile he continued: "Wa-all, I've killed my hog."

"That so? How much did he weigh?"

Farmer Evans stroked his chin whiskers meditatively and replied: "Wa-all, guess."

"'Bout three hundred," said one farmer.

"No."

"Two seventy-five?" ventured another.

"No."

"I guess about three twenty-five," said a third.

"No."

Then all together demanded: "Well, how much did he weigh?"

"Dunno. Hain't weighed him yet."

Other men kept dropping in and hugging the stove, for the day was cold and snowy outside. In came Cy Hopkins, wrapped in a big overcoat, yet almost frozen to death; but there wasn't room enough around that stove to warm his little finger.

But he didn't get mad about it; he just said to Bill Stebbins who kept the store: "Bill, got any raw oysters?"

"Yes, Cy."

"Well, just open a dozen and feed 'em to my hoss."

Well, Stebbins never was scared by an order from a man whose credit was good, as Cy's was, so he opened the oysters an' took them out, an' the whole crowd followed to see a horse eat oysters. Then Cy picked out the best seat near the stove and dropped into it as if he had come to stay, as he had.

Pretty soon the crowd came back, and the storekeeper said: "Why, Cy, your hoss won't eat them oysters."

"Won't he? Well, then, bring 'em here an' I'll eat 'em myself."

When Charley Evans and Bill Hoey traveled together, they had no end of good-natured banter between them.

Once when Hoey saw Evans mixing lemon juice and water for a gargle, he asked: "What are you doing that for, Charley?"

"Oh, for my singing."

"Suppose you put some in your ear; then maybe you'll be able to find the key."

While they were crossing the ocean, Evans came on deck one day dressed in the latest summer fashion—duck trousers, straw hat, etc.—and asked Hoey: "How do you like me, Bill?"

"Well, all you need to do now is to have your ears pierced," was the reply.

At the ship's table the waiter asked Hoey what he would have.

"Roast beef."

"How shall I cut it, sir?"

"By the ship's chart."

Evans always carried the money for both, and the two men had a fancy for wearing trousers of the same material, though of different sizes, for Evans was slighter than his partner. One day Hoey fell on hard luck. He had been to the Derby races, where a pickpocket relieved him of his watch and his money too. They were to start for America next morning, and Evans had plenty of money and return tickets also, yet Hoey was so cut up by his losses that he went to bed early and tried to drop asleep. This did not work, so after tossing for several hours, by which time Evans had retired, he got up and began to dress himself. But to his horror his figure seemed to have swelled in the night.

This was the last straw; he woke his partner and with tears in his eyes and his voice too, he said: "Charley, beside all my hard luck to-day I'm getting the dropsy."

"Bill," said Evans after a glance, "go into the other room and take off my pants!"

A certain diamond broker called on the late Charles Hoyt with a large bill.

While Hoyt was drawing a check the broker said: "Charley, a dear friend of mine was robbed yesterday."

"Is that so? Why, what did you sell him?"

The English stage is as full of jokers as ours. Wilson Barrett tells that at a "First night" his play did not seem to suit the pit, so he came before the curtain at the end of one act and asked what was the matter. The "Gods" have great freedom in English theatres, so there was much talk across the footlights between the stage and the audience; but it was stopped abruptly by a voice that said:

"Oh, go on, Wilson! This ain't no bloomin' debatin' society."

W. S. Gilbert, although not an actor, is a playwright and extremely critical. A London favorite had the best part in one of Gilbert's pieces, but the author thought him slow. Going behind the scenes after the performance, Gilbert noted that the actor's brow was perspiring, so he said:

"Well, at all events, your skin has been acting."

Gilbert can give evasive answers that cut like a knife. A player of the title part of Hamlet asked Gilbert's opinion of the performance.

"You are funny, without being vulgar," was the reply.

Forbes Robertson, who essayed the same part, asked Gilbert: "What do you think of Hamlet?"

Gilbert answered: "Wonderful play, old man; most wonderful play ever written."

E. S. Willard tells the following story of Charles Glenny, of Irving's Lyceum Company. "The Merchant of Venice" was in rehearsal, and Glenny did not repeat the lines: "Take me to the gallows, not to the font" to the liking of Irving, so the latter said in the kindly manner he always maintained at rehearsals:

"No, no, Mr. Glenny; not that way. Walk over and touch me, and say: 'Take me to the gallows, not to the font.'" The line was rehearsed several times, but unsuccessfully.

Finally Irving became discouraged and said: "Ah, well; touch me."

Irving witnessed Richard Mansfield's performance of "Richard III," in London, and by invitation went back to see the actor in his dressing-room. Mansfield had been almost exhausted, and was fanning himself, but Irving's approach revived him, and natural anticipation of a compliment from so exalted a source was absolutely stimulating.

But for the time being all Irving did was to slap Mansfield playfully on the back and exclaim in the inimitable Irving tone: "Aha? You sweat!"

"Aha! You Sweat!"

VI
A SUNNY OLD CITY

>Some Aspects of Philadelphia.—Fun in a Hospital.—"The Cripple's Palace."—An Invalid's Success in Making Other Invalids Laugh.—Fights for the Fun of Fighting.—My Rival Friends.—Boys Will Be Boys.—Cast Out of Church.—A Startling Recognition.—Some Pleasures of Attending Funerals.—How I Claimed the Protection of the American Flag.

A hospital is not a place that any one would visit if he were in search of jollity, yet some of the merriest hours of my life were spent, some years ago, in the National Surgical Institute of Philadelphia. I was one of about three hundred people, of all ages, sizes and dispositions, who were under treatment for physical defects. Most of us were practically crippled, a condition which is not generally regarded to be conductive of hilarity, yet many of us had lots of fun, and all of it was made by ourselves. I was one of the luckiest of the lot, for Mother Nature had endowed me with a faculty for finding sunshine everywhere.

Yet part of my treatment was to lie in bed, locked in braces, for hours every day, and each of these hours seemed to be several thousand minutes long. So many other boys were under similar treatment that an attendant, named Joe, was kept busy in merely taking off our appliances. These were locked, for between pain and the restiveness peculiar to boys, we would have removed them for ourselves or for one another. Joe was not a beauty, yet I distinctly remember recalling his appearance was that of an angel of light, for I best remember him in the act of loosening my braces. Whenever the surgeon in charge was absent, we would beg Joe to unlock us for "Just five minutes—just a minute"—and sometimes he would yield, after making us promise solemnly not to tell the doctor. The result recalls the story of the old darky who was seen to hammer his thumb at intervals. When asked why he did it, he replied,

"Kase it feels so good when I stop!"

To keep from thinking of my pain and helplessness, I kept looking about me for something to laugh at, and it was a rare day on which I failed to find it. When there came such a day, I had only to close my eyes and look backward a few months or years; I was sure to recall something funny. Then I would laugh. Some other sufferer would ask what was amusing me, and when I told him he would also laugh, some one would hear him and the story would have to be repeated. Soon the word got about the building that there was a little fellow in one of the rooms who was always laughing to himself, or making others laugh, so all the boys insisted on being "let in on the ground floor"—which in my case was the fourth floor. I made no objection; was there ever a man so modest that he didn't like listeners when he had anything to say? So it soon became the custom of all the boys who were not absolutely bound to their beds to congregate in my room, which would have comfortably held, not more than a dozen. Yet daily I had fifty or more around me; the earlier comers filled the chairs, later arrivals sprawled or curled on my bed, still later ones sat on the headboard and footboard, the floor accommodated others until it was packed, and the belated ones stowed themselves in the hall, within hearing distance.

'Twas a hard trip for some of them, poor fellows for there were not enough attendants to carry them all, and three flights of stairs are a hard climb for cripples. So, to prevent unnecessary pain while I was outdoors taking the air, I hung a small American flag over the stair rail opposite my door, whenever I was in; this could be seen from any of the lower halls. I learned afterward that it was the custom of royalty and other exalted personages to display a flag when they were "at home," but this did not frighten me; in memory of those hospital days, I always display a flag at my window when I am able to see my friends.

Boys are as fond as Irishmen of fighting for the mere fun of it, so we got a lot of laughing out of fist fights between some of the patients. The most popular contestants were Gott Dewey from Elmira, N. Y., and a son of Sheriff Wright of Philadelphia. Both were seriously afflicted, though they seemed not to know it. Wright was a cross-eyed paralytic, while Dewey had St. Vitus's dance and was so badly paralyzed that he had no control over his natural means of locomotion. He could not even talk intelligibly, yet he had an intellect that impressed me deeply, even at that early day. He could cope with the hardest mathematical problem that any could offer; he read much and his taste in literature and everything else was distinct and refined.

Yet, being still a boy, he enjoyed a fight, and as he and Wright were naturally antipathetic by temperament, they were always ready for a set-to. These affairs were entirely harmless, for neither could hit straighter than a girl can throw a stone. The result of their efforts was "the humor of the unexpected," and it amused us so greatly that we never noticed the pathetic side of it.

These two boys did me the honor to become very fond of me; why they did it, I don't know, unless because I never did anything in particular for Wright, yet he was always teasing Dewey, who was quite proud and self-reliant, and insisted upon doing everything for himself. That he might serve himself at table, a little elevator was made for his convenience, and I was mischievous enough to disarrange the machinery so that food intended for his mouth should reach his ear. Yet he loved me dearly and dashed at me affectionately though erratically whenever we met. I was unable to get about without crutches, so I frequently fell; if Dewey were in sight, he would hurry to my assistance, with disastrous results to both of us; often Wright would offer assistance at the same time and the two would fall over each other and me and attempt to "fight it out," while I would become helpless with laughter and the three of us would lie in a heap, until some attendant would separate the warriors and set me on my feet and crutches.

One rule of the Institute was that no patients were to leave the building on Sunday—the day on which the physicians and attendants got most liberty. To enforce this rule there was a doorkeeper named Smith. He was a dwarf, hardly four feet high, who, on Sunday would curl up in a box under his desk and wish he could have a mouthful or more of whiskey, although a little of it would put him sound asleep and leave the door unguarded against any one who cared to go out. How whiskey got into the Institute to be used upon Smith, I don't know.

I recall a Sunday when we three, Dewey, Wright and I, conceived the idea of going to church. There was a church directly across the street, so we started for it a few moments after throwing a sop of whiskey to our Cerberus. We had several mishaps on the way, due to my friend's well-meant but misdirected efforts to assist me, but passers-by kindly put us on our feet again. We got into church quite early, and passed up the aisle and entered the front pew, under the very droppings of the sanctuary. Soon after the service began a young lady at our left compelled our attention by eyeing us intently; apparently she thought us the newest thing in "The Three Graces" line. Something moved me to nudge Dewey and tell him to stop flirting with that girl. Apparently he thought I was trying to be funny, for he began laughing in his peculiar laugh, which was a sputter, with which no one familiar with it could help being amused, so Wright laughed too, after which it was impossible for me to keep quiet. We really were reverent little chaps, so we tried hard to suppress ourselves, but—boys will be boys. Suddenly we three exploded as one; we could hear tittering around us, the minister stopped in the middle of an eloquent period, raised his glasses, and I shall never forget his pained expression of astonishment as he caught sight of us for the first time. Suddenly there appeared a platoon of deacons, two of whom attached themselves to each of us, and we were conducted down the aisle, facing an array of hymn-books, behind which the congregation were trying to hide their own laughter. The next day the church sent the Institute a polite but earnest request that no more cripples be allowed to attend service in that church.

"There appeared a Platoon of Deacons."

After leaving the Institute I lost sight of Dewey, though I never forgot his hearty way of greeting me whenever he met me, a heartiness which caused him to tumble all over me and compel me to put out my arm to save him from falling. Five years ago on reaching a Philadelphia church whose members I had been engaged to "entertain," the committee of arrangements met me and said they wished to prepare me for the unusual appearance of their chairman. He had endowed the church, they told me, and was almost idolized by the people for his many noble qualities of head and heart, yet he was a paralytic and his visage was shocking at first sight. Suddenly the chairman himself entered the room and I saw my old friend Gott Dewey. At the same instant he recognized me; he dashed at me in his old way; my arm instinctively caught him as it had done hundreds of times before; the committee supposing I was frightened, endeavored to separate us, but we weren't easy to handle, so there was a close mix up, while, in which, the dear old boy with tears streaming down his cheeks, endeavored to explain that we were fast friends. Then he told me he had read my book "People I've Smiled With," and been so greatly amused by it that he had suggested my engagement to entertain his church people, yet he had never imagined I was the Wilder boy of "The Cripple's Palace."

It took him fifteen minutes to say all this and conquer his emotion; then he wanted to go on the platform and tell his people about me and what old friends we were. I realized that if he were to do it, I would never reach the platform myself, so I persuaded him to let me tell them the story. He consented, but insisted on accompanying me, and tearfully confirming every thing I said, so with him beside me, for "local color," I got along so well that there was not a dry eye in the house. It was an inexpressible relief to me to set everybody laughing afterward, for I never needed a "bracing up" more than on that night.

Dewey had always longed to be a lawyer and I learned that he had succeeded in gratifying this ambition, in spite of his heavy physical handicap: he became so able as a counselor that he gained a large practice and was specially skilful at preparing briefs for his partner to take into court. He was held in high honor for his charitable work and for many years led a successful, useful and happy life; but not long after our unexpected meeting he was complained of as a public nuisance and was actually arrested on this charge. His appearance and manner were really terrifying to people that did not know him, for in trying to avoid collision with passers-by his lack of control often caused him to act as if about to strike. The magistrate, before whom he was arraigned expressed extreme sympathy, but insisted that he keep out of the streets except when in a carriage or when properly attended, and poor Dewey took the affair so deeply to heart, that afterward he kept himself almost secluded from the world.

Mention of Philadelphia almost always suggests graveyards to me, not that the city prides itself on being "well laid-out," but because I have visited all its cemeteries many times. When I left the Surgical Institute I boarded with a woman whose husband kept a large livery stable. I made friends of the drivers, and, as I was still under treatment and could not get about much, they would kindly give me an airing, whenever they were engaged for funerals, which was almost daily. This often meant an all day trip; my motherly landlady would put up a substantial lunch for me and the drivers granted me special privileges; that is, I was generally taken on the seat of the driver of the carriage which followed the hearse. The one that "carried the criers," to use the stable parlance. It would not seem a cheerful way of spending a day, but I was always very much alive, and the drivers were as cheerful as if going to a wedding, and, while the ceremony at the grave was in progress, I ate my lunch with the hunger sauce that a long drive always supplies, and in summer I could generally find some flowers in the path to take home to my landlady. Besides, some of the cemeteries were so well kept that they were as sightly as gardens, which reminds me of a story that I once inflicted on the Clover Club of Philadelphia, as follows:

"While dining at my hotel yesterday, I noticed that the water looked muddy, so I complained to the waiter. He admitted that it looked bad, but said it was really very good water.

"He Said it was Very Good Water."

"'But,' I continued, 'they tell me that the water here passes through a graveyard (Laurel Hill Cemetery) before reaching the people.'

"'That's right, sir,' the waiter replied. 'But it's a first-class graveyard; only the best people are buried there.'"

I have traveled much in foreign countries, but Philadelphia is the only place in which I was compelled to beg the protection of the American flag. I had been engaged by Mr. John Wanamaker to "say something" to his great Sunday-school on two consecutive evenings. Being a New Yorker, I did not care to spend the intervening hours in Philadelphia, so after leaving the platform the first evening, I took the ten o'clock train for home. As haste was necessary, I merely changed my evening coat and vest for street clothes. In New York next day, I changed my black trousers for gray, attended to so much business that I had to take a late afternoon train, and did not realize until it was almost time to go on the platform, in a "swallow-tail" coat that I had no black trousers. Worse still my figure was such that I could not be fitted from any clothing store in the city. For a moment my invention was at a standstill, but the people were not, and the hall was filling rapidly.

I consulted the committee hastily, and though they were greatly amused by my suggestion, they acted upon it promptly: they moved a table to the centre of the platform, draped it with the stars and stripes, and all the people on the platform arranged themselves, so that I could be unseen as I passed behind them to the table, where only my coat and vest could be seen, the objectionable trousers being hidden by my country's flag.

Small wonder that I have a merry remembrance of Philadelphia.

VII
MY FIRST TRIP TO LONDON

Large Hopes vs. Small Means.—At the Savage Club.—My First Engagement.—Within an Ace of Losing It.—Alone in a Crowd.—A Friendly Face to the Rescue.—The New York Welcome to a Fine Fellow.—One English Way With Jokes.—People Who are Slow to Laugh.—Disturbing Elements.—Cold Audiences.—Following a Suicide.

When first I visited London I carried large hopes and a small purse and the latter became so much smaller in the course of time, that I had to live on next to nothing; to be exact, I restricted myself to fifty cents a day. For seventy-five cents a week I had a little room in Tottenham Court Road—a very narrow-minded room indeed, with furnishings to match. Cold, damp weather was the only guest or companion I had, and the room's carpet served two purposes; it covered the floor by day and the bed at night. From the tiny window there was a long vista of chimney-pots, which, next to an array of ready-made coffins, offer as disquieting a spectacle as a homesick boy can gaze upon. The boy Chatterton came to my mind many times in those days, and although I hoped his fate would not be mine, I nevertheless learned at times how annoying hunger may be when it passes the point of anticipation of "a square meal."

One treasure did much to sustain me; it was a card, given me by an American friend before I left home, introducing me to the Savage Club, which is similar to the Lotos Club of New York. I had the freedom of the Savage at all times, and was allowed to have my letters addressed there—a privilege which literally "saved my face," for I would never have dared to pose as an entertainer if my address had been Tottenham Court Road. I had good clothes and I kept a stiff upper lip, so no member of the club knew of my financial straits. I was careful to refrain from forcing myself upon any of the club members who had been so kind as to notice me, yet dinner invitations from some of these good fellows were all that saved my slender bank balance from extinction.

Despite my own economy and the hospitality of others there came a day when Melancholy—with a large M,—threatened to mark me for her own, for my sole assets, excepting my clothing, were six dollars and my return ticket; the latter I could not convert into cash without burning my bridge behind me—and the Atlantic is too wide for a return trip by raft. Just as this crisis had made me as miserable as any man could be, I received the following dispatch from a club member who probably had been present at some of the volunteer entertainments I had given at the Savage.

"What are your terms? Come to-night; No. 5 Princess Gate."

I quickly wired back: "Will come. Terms ten guineas."

For the remainder of the day I stayed away from the club, and tormented myself with fears that I had named too high a price, though I had always believed there was wisdom in Emerson's advice—"Hitch your wagon to a star." I resolved to go that night to 5 Princess Gate; then, if they had canceled the engagement, I could honestly say I had not received notice.

In the evening I made a careful toilet, using my last bit of clean linen, and took a twopenny 'bus to my destination. The powdered footman who opened the door said he would bring his Lordship's secretary to see me. The secretary came in, much embarrassed, and said he had wired me that other arrangements had been made.

"I have been so busy all day," I replied, "that I've not called at the club; consequently I did not get your message. What was the trouble?—my terms?"

"We have engaged a different entertainer," he replied evasively.

"But, you see," I said, with my heart in my mouth, which had need of something more edible, "your telegram this morning told me to come, so my evening is lost. As I am here, suppose I go up and do what I can. As to my fee—oh, I'm quite willing to leave that to his lordship."

"I told him many stories hoping he would not notice my appetite."

Just then I heard his lordship's voice saying, "Come in, Mr. Wilder." He seemed to have grasped the situation, and with the tact and courtesy which is never lacking in English gentlemen, he quickly made me feel entirely at ease. He also offered me refreshments, and as I had not dined, I gladly accepted. That I might not be alone at table, he kindly waited with me. I told him many stories, hoping he would not notice my appetite, but I noticed it myself so persistently that I felt that his every glance said distinctly:

"You poor little devil, how hungry you are!"

But I persisted; I was conscious of a need to be well fortified, for I had heard all sorts of stories about entertaining at social functions in England—stories of arrays of old ladies in low-necked gowns displaying more bones than beauty,—of a subdued patter of gloved hands in place of real applause—of "the stony British stare," which, really, is never encountered in society, so I felt like a soldier about to face fearful odds. I was so wrought upon by my fears that when I did appear it seemed to me that there was not in that great drawing-room a single sympathetic face at which I might play; all appeared to wear an expression which said:

"Now, then;—make us laugh if you can."

I began to feel as if I was looking into the rear end of an ice wagon, but suddenly my eye found a man's face which filled me with courage—a face full of kindness, humor and sympathy. It seemed to say:

"My poor boy, you're in hard luck, and I'm going to give you all the help I can. If there's an excuse for a laugh, you're going to get it."

My heart swelled and went out to him; although I had much to think of at the moment, business being business and I about to put my wedge into it for the first time in an English drawing-room, I mentally vowed that if ever I met that man again he should know what a tower of strength he had been to me. I "spread myself," I "laid myself out," and was told afterward that I had succeeded. My own view-point of success was reached next morning, when I received his lordship's check.

Several weeks afterward, at a dinner given to Henry Irving, I saw again the kind face that had been a world of encouragement to me. At the earliest possible opportunity I went over to him and said:

"I want to thank you for helping me at a very trying moment."

Through forgetfulness or modesty he appeared not to remember the affair, so I detailed the circumstance to him. He expressed delight at having been of any service to me, and confessed that he was a fellow professional, and could therefore imagine my feelings when first face to face with an English audience. I asked him what he was doing; he replied that he was at the Princess Theatre with Mr. Wilson Barrett. I begged him to let me knew his whereabouts whenever he came to the United States, so that I might renew my expressions of gratitude and be of any possible service to him. He promised, but just as I was taking leave of him it occurred to me that I did not even know his name, so I asked for it. He replied:

"My name is Willard—Edward S. Willard."

We became quite close friends in the course of years, although Mr. Willard did not come to America until 1891. Soon after his arrival I gave a breakfast at Delmonico's in his honor and ransacked the city and vicinity for fine fellows to meet him. Among the guests were Gen. W. T. Sherman, Col. Robert G. Ingersoll, George W. Childs, editor of the Philadelphia *Ledger*; Whitelaw Reid, editor-in-chief of the New York *Tribune*; Hugh J. Grant, Mayor of New York; Chauncey M. Depew, president of the New York Central Railway Company and his secretary Captain Henry Du Val; Hon. Daniel Dougherty, the most brilliant member of the Philadelphia bar; theatre managers Augustin Daly, A. M. Palmer, Frank Sanger, Henry E. Abbey, and Daniel Frohman; Joseph I. C. Clarke, editor of the *Morning Journal*; Foster Coates, editor of the *Mail and Express*; St. Clair McKelway, editor of the Brooklyn *Union*; J. M. Stoddart, manager of *Lippincott's Magazine*; Chester A. Lord, managing editor of the New York *Sun*; Bradford Merrill, managing editor of the New York *World*; Arthur Bowers managing editor of New York *Tribune*; Joseph Howard, Jr., America's most noted newspaper correspondent; Col. T. P. Ochiltree, the world's most effective impromptu story teller; John Russell Young, editor, librarian of the congressional library and ex-minister to China; Major Moses P. Handy, journalist, club president and United States Commissioner to the Paris exposition; William Edgar Nye (Bill Nye, the humorist); Sam Sothern, brother of E. H. Sothern the actor; W. J. Arkell, manager of *Puck* and *Leslie's Weekly*; Harrison Gray Fiske, editor *Dramatic Mirror*; Col. W. F. Cody ("Buffalo Bill"); W. J. Florence, the comedian, Henry Watterson, editor of the Louisville *Courier-Journal* and also the most quoted editor in America, and Joseph Hatton the noted English author.

Toward the end of the breakfast I said:

"Gentlemen, I should like to tell you the story of a poor boy and an actor and the kindness the actor showed the poor boy." I then related, in the third person, the story of my first evening as an entertainer in London, and concluded with:

"Gentleman, I am that poor boy, and the actor, whose kindness I can never forget, is our guest, Mr. Edward S. Willard." And straightway the entire company rose and let Willard know what they thought of that sort of chap.

After I had broken the ice in London by Mr. Willard's aid, as already described, I got along quite swimmingly, and felt so at ease that I imagined I never could find myself unable to capture whatever audience I might face. But there is no accounting for audiences; occasionally they take an entertainer right to their hearts, read his stories in his face and have their applause ready for us the instant the point appears. A day or two later the entertainer may appear before a lot of men and women of intelligent appearance without eliciting a smile. These unaccountable differences are not peculiar to either England or America. Every summer when I revisit England, some old acquaintance is sure to say, "Mr. Wilder, those stories you told last year are awfully funny." It has really taken him about a year to get at the points of the various tales; he doesn't lack appreciation of humor, but he is so accustomed to having it served in only one way that he is puzzled when it appears in a new form. One day I told an English audience about New York's fire department and its methods; great interest was manifested, so I ventured to tell the old story of a fire in an India rubber factory. This factory was a large, tall building, and when the alarm of fire was given one of the employees found himself on the top floor, with burning stairs under him. His only chance was to jump, but the pavement was so far below his windows that death seemed inevitable. Suddenly he bethought himself of the elastic properties of rubber, of which the room was full; could he envelop himself with it he might jump and strike the sidewalk softly! So he donned rubber coats, belts, diving suits and everything else he could find, until he made the serious mistake of putting on too much, for when he jumped he rebounded from the pavement again and again and continued to do so, for five days, when a merciful police officer came along and shot the poor fellow to save him from starving to death.

"A merciful police officer came along and shot the poor fellow."

About half an hour after I told this veracious story one of my audience came to me and asked:

"Mr. Wilder, do you think that police officer was justified?"

He was no worse than the person, to be found in both England and America, who sees a joke so slowly that his laugh comes in when there is nothing to laugh at. I recall a woman of this kind whose belated laugh was so immense when it did arrive that I stopped and said:

"Madam, if you will kindly keep that laugh till a little later, it will do me lots of good."

Some people who have been of my audience meet me afterward and proceed to "take the gilt off of the gingerbread" in an amusing fashion—if I am sensible enough to take it that way. Once I encountered one of the blundering old chaps who mean well, yet invariably make a break and he said:

"Mr. Wilder, there was one very good thing among those stories you told."

I was disconcerted for a moment, but recovering myself I said:

"Well, that's better than missing the point of all of them."

At one of my private entertainments I was "making good" and was keeping my audience in continuous merriment, but my hostess begged me to cease making them laugh and say something sad and pathetic, so that they might catch their breath and rest their aching sides.

"My dear madam," I replied, "I am never sad or pathetic—I mean, not intentionally."

With a properly developed sense of humor one can sometimes bring a laugh out of disconcerting surroundings. While I was talking to an audience at Flint, Mich., one night, the lights suddenly went out but I succeeded in saying:

"That's too bad. Now I'm afraid you won't be able to see through my jokes."

One evening in the course of an engagement I was playing at the Orpheum in Brooklyn; one of the boxes was occupied by a quartette who had evidently been drinking "not wisely, but too well." They were giving the audience the benefit of their conversation and even sharing the honors of the entertainment with the ladies and gentlemen on the bill, much to the annoyance of these, for the disturbance was interfering seriously with good work. I had been watching from the wings and determined I would not submit to such distraction, so when I went on I said:

"Ladies and gentlemen, it is an oft-repeated remark that it takes all kinds of people to make a world. Some people in an audience are so sensitive that they are affected by any unusual conditions or surroundings. For instance, if they find themselves among ladies and gentlemen they are so elated by the fact that their conduct has every appearance of intoxication—but it really is not intoxication, though it may look that way." My performance, which followed immediately, was not disturbed, nor was that of any one who followed me.

Every entertainer knows what terrible up-hill work it is to stand before a cold audience. Cold that affects the body is bliss in comparison with the awful atmosphere that creeps chillingly into one's soul and the very marrow of his bones. How an audience can get into such a condition and become so appalling an influence passes comprehension, for not all the men and women present can have become dyspeptic on the same day, or had their consciences awakened at the same hour, or simultaneously "gone broke" or seen themselves as others saw them. Sometimes I've thought it came of the actual atmosphere of the house, for there are theatres, halls, churches and parlors that are never properly aired unless hailstorms or hoodlums chance to break the windows.

But all such speculation is getting away from the audience, whereas that is the one thing the entertainer daren't do, much though he may wish to. He is "stuck" for a given period, and he is reminded of trying to climb slippery mountains of ice in the fairy tales of childhood's sunny hour, and the parallel continues, for the chill—the reserve, is more often melted by some happy impromptu than by conscientious work.

I recall a time in Pittsburg when I struck the afore-mentioned Polar current through no fault of my own or of the audience. It was the custom of the house to begin the evening with a play and follow with a vaudeville performance. The play on the occasion referred to was "Captain Swift," in which the hero was a charming rascal who always took an audience by the heart, even when he ended the play by killing himself. It was my misfortune to follow the play and find the audience in a very low state of mind which, in turn, threw a wet blanket upon me and my work. After laboring a few minutes I said:

"Ladies and gentlemen, I've often followed a prayer, and sometimes followed a hearse, but this is the first time I ever followed a suicide." This touch just tipped the balance—lifted the cloud, squeezed the water out of the blanket, made the audience mine and kept it so while I held the stage.

At the Orpheum in San Francisco I was received so kindly that my stay was extended to three weeks. San Francisco audiences are very responsive, except on Sunday evenings; then, for some Frisco reason undiscoverable by the eastern man, they are usually cold and the entertainer has to cut ice. On my last Sunday evening there a section of Greenland's Icy Mountains seemed to have come in collision with a cold-storage warehouse just before I appeared, for the audience was as unresponsive as a cart load of frozen clams. I worked over them a few moments as earnestly as a life-saver over a person rescued from drowning, but to no avail, so I stopped and said:

"Now I've got you nice and quiet, just have a good long sleep while I go out and leave a call for you." Then I tiptoed off of the stage so as not to rouse the sleepers. This started a current of warm good nature; they called me back and for the rest of the performance there was perfect understanding and sympathy between them and me.

VIII
EXPERIENCES IN LONDON

Customs and Climate Very Unlike Our Own.—No Laughter in Restaurants.—Clever Cabbies.—Oddities in Fire-fighting.—The "Rogues' Gallery" in Scotland Yard.—"Petticoat Lane."—A Cemetery for Pet Dogs.—Dogs Who are Characters.—The Professional Toast-master.—Solemn After-dinner Speakers.—An Autograph Table-cloth.—American Brides of English Husbands.

So many London customs seem strange to an American that I venture to mention a few experiences of my own by way of preparation, for no American knows when he may be nominated for the presidency or get a chance to go to Europe.

The first thing to impress a person from this side of the Atlantic is the climate, which is generally depressing to any one accustomed to the dazzling sunshine, brilliant skies and champagne quality of our atmosphere. Everything seems heavy and solemn by comparison, and life appears to be a serious matter to all whom one meets, although the truth is that the English enjoy life heartily and give ten times as much attention to sports and amusements as we do.

I went one day into a restaurant where a great many people were dining, yet absolute silence prevailed, instead of the buzz of chatter and laughter of a French or American restaurant. I asked a waiter,

"Doesn't any one ever laugh here?"

"Yes, sir," he replied. "Sometimes we 'ave complaints, sir."

But there is so much of interest in even the ordinary street sights that a visitor soon forgets smoke, dampness and gloom. The first natives to accost an American are the "cabbies," and they are a never-failing source of amusement to me. They abound in natural wit, and are past-masters of sarcasm. One of the sharpest bits I ever heard was told about an old cabby and one of his younger fellows. The former was a master of whip and rein; he boasted that he knew every foot of London and declared that although he had been in many tight places he had never failed to drive out smoothly. One day, however, he lost control of his horse and ran into a young cabby's outfit. The younger man looked him over condescendingly, contemptuously, and then asked,

"Well? An' 'ow do *you* like London?"

A friend of mine once took a cab drawn by an animal which was bony in the extreme. The driver was hailed by the Jehu of a passing cab with,

"Oi saiy, Bill, I see yer goin' to 'ave a new 'orse."

"'Oo told yer so?"

"W'y, I see y've got the framework there."

Not all the quick-tongued cabbies are professionals. At one time it was a fad of young "bloods" in London to drive cabs, apparently for the purpose of enriching their slang vocabulary by exchanging remarks with "regulars" whom they could provoke into freedom of speech. Sometimes decently born and fairly educated young men from the rural districts, who have handled horses at home and know no one in London whom they would be ashamed to face from a driver's seat, try cab-driving as a business. They can hire a horse and cab for five shillings a day; London fares are small and some days they are few, but many men "tip" the drivers, especially those who say smart things that appear to be impromptu, so amateur cabbies sometimes make much more than a living.

London's fire-fighting service interests an American by its differences from our own. The fire-plugs do not resemble old-fashioned cannon, turned upside down, as ours do; they are so unnoticeable that their whereabouts must be indicated by lamp-post signs like this:—"Fire-plug four feet to the right and three feet to the rear." Instead of using whistles, the London engines have a string of sleigh-bells on one of the horses, and by way of further warning the men on the engine keep up a constant shout of "Hoy! Hoy! Hoy!" The engines do not respond as quickly to an alarm as ours; it generally takes them two minutes to get under way, though the firemen are a "fit" looking lot. I was told they were selected entirely from ex-sailors of the naval service. To assist the engines' crews there are many auxiliaries, who sleep and almost live in small red houses on wheels; these portable houses are numerous in the more thickly populated portions of the city, where fires are most likely to occur and extra firemen be needed.

At convenient corners are kept, also on wheels, the portable fire-escapes:— mere shafts or chutes of canvas on wooden framework. In case of fire in the upper part of an inhabited building, the top of the escape is pushed to a window, and the inmates are expected to save themselves by going head first down the inclined chute, clinging to the framework of the sides to keep from descending too rapidly. Of course in a city of lofty apartment houses and "sky-scraper" office buildings such a contrivance would be almost useless, but in London a house of more than three stories is a rarity. "Running to fires" is as popular with some Londoners as it was in New York before fire alarms reached the dozen-a-day mark. The Duke of Sutherland enjoyed attending fires; he would have his private carriage follow the engines, and frequently he was accompanied by the Prince of Wales.

Scotland Yard, mentioned in every English detective story, is an interesting place to visit; it is the London equivalent of our Police Department's "Central Office." I was shown a "Rogues' Gallery" there which was quite as large and appalling as our own. In photographing a criminal the London police make assurance doubly sure by placing a mirror to catch his profile, which is taken, with his front face, by a single snap. To be still more thorough they have the sitters spread his hands on his chest, for hands, being hard to disguise, are useful tell-tales. Thumb impressions complete a record which the criminal regards with far more discomfort than his evil deeds ever give him.

Petticoat Lane is not a section of the police department, though the officials wish it might be, for as it is a recognized "stand" of hucksters, the thieves flock there to sell their ill-gotten wares, so one may see "Fagins" and "Artful Dodgers" in plenty. Their best customers are men of their own kind—thieves with enough business sense to know where certain kinds of stolen property can be resold to advantage. Jewelry is the principal stock-in-trade, and it is carried in small boxes, resembling cigar-boxes, hung from the neck. When the coast is clear of policemen, the thieves lift the lid long enough for a peep at the contents. I was piloted through "the lane" by a special officer from Scotland Yard and in an underground passage we came upon a score or more of the light-fingered gentry. Unfortunately the officer was recognized, word was passed down the line, everything that might have aroused suspicion was secreted and the entire crowd gazed at us with an affected innocence which was transparent enough to be laughable.

The legitimate trades in Petticoat Lane are more interesting to an American, for they have some business ways which are amusing—even startling. An orange-dealer will drop his fruit in hot water once in a while; this makes it swell to almost twice its natural size and look smooth and glossy. The next wagon to the orange man may be full of second-hand clothing; the dealer will not allow a would-be purchaser to "try on" a coat or vest, for fear he may run away with it, but he will put the garment on his own wife for inspection; the result is often a picture funny enough to print. Theatrical people often go there for costumes for "character" parts; apparently some kinds of English clothing last forever, for in Petticoat Lane may be seen fabrics and fashions and trimmings that look antiquated enough to have come over with William the Conqueror. Some of the hucksters' carts are decorated with suggestive signs, such as, "Oh, mother, how cheap these eggs are!"

In a corner of Hyde Park I chanced to see a little graveyard; everything about it was little. The mounds were small, the headstones tiny, and little children were decorating the graves with flowers. On inquiry I learned that it was a dogs' cemetery, but instead of laughing I was touched by the mental picture of heavy-hearted boys and girls going there with floral tributes to departed playfellows. A little girl who was passing noted that one grave was bare, and I heard her say to her nurse:

"That must have been a bad doggie buried there."

"Why?" the nurse inquired.

"Because he has no flowers on his grave."

Almost every part of London has its homely "character." Near St. Martin's Lane, off Charing Cross, can be seen every day a blind sailor who sits knitting small fishing-nets. In front of him sits his Irish terrier with a cup in his mouth, and passers-by amuse themselves by throwing pennies for the dog to catch in his cup, as he always does. When he has caught several he empties the cup into his owner's hand and returns to business at the old stand. This goes on till evening, when the dog guides his owner home through the crowded streets.

One interesting London dog is called Nelson, because he accidentally lost a leg at the base of the Nelson column in Trafalgar Square. He makes his home in Seven Dials, where he begs for a living, and gets many pennies from his admirers. Instead of giving the money to any one he hides it; whenever he is hungry he goes to his treasury, gets a coin and takes it to a butcher or baker; he knows, too, how much he should get in return and he will not leave the shop till he has received full value for his money.

The professional toast-master is a London institution that America has not adopted. His services are required at the cost of a sovereign, at every public dinner, and his qualifications are pomposity and a loud, deep, resonant voice. Around his neck he wears a big silver chain from which hangs a silver plate inscribed T. M., and when he exclaims, "We will drink a bumper to 'Is Gracious Majesty the King," it is with a voice that suggests an earthquake announcing its exit from the bowels of the earth. After the presiding officer has indulged in the usually introductory and airy persiflage, it is the duty of the T. M. to introduce the speaker, which he does with a sweep of his arm that is expected to subdue any noisy applause by the guests.

"'Is Gracious Majesty the King!"

English after-dinner speakers have little or no humor, but they are extremely earnest in their remarks. They incline more to argument than amusement. Occasionally one will indulge in a pun which has the sanctity of long usage—a pun that an American could not get off without a blush, and a turn of his face to the wall, but the hearers like it, so no one else should complain. The English recognize and admit the American's superiority as an after-dinner speaker. I heard Mr. Beerbohm Tree say, in the course of a speech at the Clover Club (Philadelphia),

"Englishmen can handle horses and Americans their tongues."

But there are exceptions to every rule, even regarding dinners and after-dinner speaking. London contains some men as clever and witty as any in the world, and when these fine fellows dine together there is no formality about the board nor any heavy talk.

Mr. Henry Lucy, who has been called the "Mark Twain of England," recently visited this country with Mrs. Lucy, renewing old friendships and forming new ones. The Lucys give delightful dinners at their home in Ashley Gardens, Victoria Street, as I have often had occasion to know, and the guests they gather about them would be welcomed by the cleverest men and women anywhere. For special occasions the Lucys use a table-cloth profusely ornamented with the autographs of many brilliant men who have dined with them, for it is only as a guest that one may write his name on this sacred bit of linen. Many of the names are household words in America, one of which held my eye for an entire evening; it was that of Charles Dickens. It was over the Lucy table that Burnand, editor of *Punch*, and W. S. Gilbert had their oft-quoted encounter:

"I suppose you often have good things sent in by outsiders?" said Gilbert.

"Frequently," Burnand replied.

"Then why don't you print them?"

A question frequently asked of late is whether the marriages of American girls to English husbands result happily. My own observation has satisfied me that they generally do. English girls are educated to be good housewives and mothers, but their childhood and early girlhood is usually spent in the nursery, without much association with adults, so when they are thrust into society they are likely to be shy, if not awkward, and have little or nothing to say. But the American girl is "one of the family" from her infancy; she is as much a companion of her father as her brother is, and she knows her brother's friends as well as those of her elder sister. She acquires quickness of thought and speech, vivacity and cleverness, and can be companionable without overstepping the bounds of strict propriety.

If an English gentleman longs for a wife who will also be his "chum," who will enjoy his sports with him and be a jolly good fellow, which is only another name for companion—who is competent to amuse and entertain, he cannot easily find her in England except in a class which would preclude his offering her his name, but if he is so lucky as to marry an American girl he has not only a model wife and housekeeper but a companion as well.

Mill put the garment on his wife.

Just one more mention of London, for the sake of that touch of nature that makes the whole world kin. Down by the East India dock is a hospital on the wall of which appears the following request, "Will drivers please walk their horses?" Although heavy traffic passes the building, much noise is avoided if horses are not urged beyond a walk. The drivers are a rather rough lot, like drivers anywhere, but they carefully comply with the request; their knowledge of what it means is more effective than a platoon of police could be. The gratitude of the hospital authorities and patients is expressed by an inscription at the other end of the building—"Thank you, drivers."

"We cannot chain the eagle;

And we dare not chain the dove;

But every gate that's barred by hate

Is opened wide by love."

IX
"LUCK" IN STORY-TELLING

The Real Difference Between Good Luck and Bad.—Good Luck with Stories Presupposes a Well-stored Memory.—Men Who Always Have the Right Story Ready.—Mr. Depew.—Bandmaster Sousa's Darky Stories.—John Wanamaker's Sunday-school Stories.—Gen. Horace Porter's Tales That go to the Spot.—The Difference Between Parliament and Congress.

The difference between good luck and bad luck amounts generally to the difference between the men who are said to have the one or the other. Some men are always waiting for something to turn up: others make sure of it by taking something—anything—from a spade to their wits, and digging it up. Anywhere in the country one may see holding down chairs in the store, or in the city lounging at tables in bar-rooms, a knot of men who were born with average brains, yet they will drone dismally of successful men whom they know or have heard of:

"Smith became a preacher at twelve thousand a year."

"Jones dropped into a Supreme Court Judgeship."

"Brown stumbled on a business chance that made him a millionaire."

"Well, there's nothing like luck"—and they go on sitting still waiting for it, and can't imagine why it never comes their way. I once chanced to mention Chauncey Depew's name in the hearing of a crowd of this kind, and a voice replied:

"There's a lucky man for you! Why, whenever he hears of anything, it is just his luck to have a story that goes to the spot as quick as a bullet from a gun."

This sort of "luck," like the other instances referred to, is the inevitable outcome of the man and his ways. There are jokes for every situation, as there are keys for every lock; but the man who lets a good joke go in one ear and out of the other is like him who puts his keys into a pocket with a hole in it, and then grumbles that he can't unlock his doors. Jokes are like dollars: when you have some that are not needed at the time, it is better to stow them away for future use than to drop them where they can't be found in case of need.

I can recall from my own experience but one case of sheer luck in story-telling. While dining at an Englishman's magnificent place one summer, some peaches were served. As the English climate is too cool to ripen peaches, these had been grown on the side of a wall and under glass. They were superb in size and color yet they had small stones and little flavor. When my host told me of the care that had been lavished on them—they must have cost him a dollar each—my mind went back to the peach season at home, so I said to him:

"Peaches that would make your mouth water and send tears of joy chasing one another down your cheeks are to-day piled high on barges beside the wharves of New York and selling at a dollar a basket, with from one to two hundred peaches in each basket."

I made this truthful statement in a matter-of-fact way, which was all it called for; but my host looked at me in amazement, then laughed heartily and said:

"Well, you Americans have always been remarkable for the stories you tell."

To revert to Mr. Depew, he can tell a new story every day of the year, and add two or three by way of good measure; but their newness is generally in the patness of their application. He is so able at this sort of thing that he can turn a story against the man who tells it. But he confesses gleefully to having been caught once in the same manner. He was billed to make a speech somewhere up the state, and when he arrived the editor of the local paper called at his hotel to argue politics with him. The editor quoted newspaper statements frequently to support his arguments, but Depew replied:

"Oh, you can't believe everything the newspapers say."

"The editor of the local paper called at his hotel."

After the speech-making ended, the editor and Mr. Depew met again, in the centre of a crowd of listeners.

"Well, my friend," the genial Chauncey asked, "what did you think of my speech?"

The editor hesitated a moment before he inquired solemnly: "Are you the genuine Chauncey M. Depew?"

"Certainly! Do you doubt it?"

Again the editor hesitated. He regarded the speaker as if he was sizing him up, and asked: "Are you the man all the newspapers have been saying is the finest speaker, the greatest talker, the sharpest stumper and the brightest wit before the public?"

Depew modestly blushed at this array of compliments; but replied: "I guess I am he. But why do you ask?"

"Oh, because one can't believe everything the newspapers say."

And Depew made haste to shake hands with the editor and call it square.

Mr. Depew's humorous speeches read so well that nobody misses one of them if he can help it; but it is impossible for cold type to suggest the inimitable manner with which they are given. A mature maiden woman once called upon him at an hour when his time was worth about a dollar a second and asked his advice about buying a certain bit of real estate. He evasively answered that there were two things of which he knew absolutely nothing: they were women and real estate.

This amused her so greatly that she lingered instead of going away, and to prolong her stay she asked about a mutual acquaintance: "Where is Mr. Blank, Mr. Depew?"

"He is still in the city."

"Does he stammer as much as he did?"

"Oh, yes; worse, I believe."

"Strange he never married."

"No, it was not strange, my dear madam. Blank courted a lovely girl—he told me of it years afterward—and this is the way he proposed." Then Mr. Depew looked soulfully at his visitor and stammered: "'D-d-d-dear a-a-angel, I l-l-l-love y-y-you!' And the woman replied: 'You need not proceed further, Mr. Blank. I do not care to be wooed on the instalment plan.'" But the visitor had fled too rapidly to get the benefit of the joke.

Bandmaster Sousa is one of the "lucky" story-tellers, for he can always cap an improbable story with a bigger one. After listening to an extraordinary yarn about some man's appetite, and another about unquestioning confidence in another man's directions, he "covered" both with the following, which he attributed to a Southern negro:

"Down on our fahm we'ze got a man by de name o' Jim. Now, Jim's de champion ham-eater of all de country roun'. Unc' Henry hed cha'ge o' de fahm, an' ev'ybody 'spected Unc' Henry, an' when Unc' Henry tol' any of us to do anythin' we jus' done it, 'ithout stoppin' to ask any questions, 'cause we had conf'dence in him. We knowed he wouldn't ever tell us to do anythin' dat we hadn't orter.

"But dat Jim—w'y, folks come f'om all de country roun', jes' to see Jim eat ham, fo' de way he could tuck ham away was amazin'; it suttinly was. How you would laugh to see Jim a-settin' by de fence one day, a-eatin' one ham after another, like ez ef dey was cakes or biscuits! 'Twas 'ez easy to him as pickin' teeth, an' he'd got down eight hams, an' de ninth was a follerin', but I reckon it wuz f'om a middlin' old hawg, for some gris'le got in his throat, an' choked him an' stopped his breath, so we wuz a-feared dat we wuz a-goin' to lose Jim.

"But up got Unc' Henry sort o' easy-like, an' he went over to de fence—dey was a lot o' slabs on top o' de fence—and he tuk a slab, an' he walk t'ward Jim, an' he sez: 'Jim, git down on all fours!' Dat slab looked mighty big, it did, an' right in front o' Jim was a big pile o' stones; but Jim had conf'dence in Unc' Henry, like ev'ybody did, so he got down on all fours an' waited, an' de gris'le in his throat, why, dat waited too. An' Unc' Henry pahted Jim's coat-tails, an' histed de slab, an' fetched it down wid a mighty swish, an' give Jim a hit, an' Jim went head first onto dat pile o' stones; but he had conf'dence in Unc' Henry so he knowed he wouldn't be knocked through de stones, but would stop ez soon ez he hit 'em—his conf'dence in Unc' Henry was dat great. An' when he struck dem stones dat piece o' gris'le 'lowed it had bizness somewhar else. An' Jim riz up an' hollered 'Gimme anudder ham!'"

Depew—Porter—Wilder—Sousa—Wanamaker

It will amaze millions of John Wanamaker's customers to know that the man who is so busy that they can never get a glimpse of him unless they attend his church is an industrious teller of stories and always has the "luck"—though that is not his name for it—to have the right story for any situation. That most of his yarns are spun in Sunday-school does not make them any the less good. I wish Sunday-school teachers had told stories when I was a boy, and I will bet Bibles to buttons that if teachers were practically instructed in story-telling, all the Sunday-school rooms would have to be enlarged to hold the increase of attendants.

But I was speaking of John Wanamaker. While reproving some of his Sunday-school pupils for laughing at a deaf boy's wrong answers to misunderstood questions, he said:

"Boys, it isn't right to laugh at any one's affliction. Besides, you never know when your own words may be turned against you. I once knew a deaf man—let us call him Brown—who was disposed to stinginess and to getting every dollar he could out of everybody and everything. He never married; but he was very fond of society, so one day he felt compelled to give a banquet to the many ladies and gentlemen whose guest he had been.

"They were amazed that his purse-strings had been unloosed so far, and they thought he deserved encouragement, so it was arranged that he should be toasted. One of the most daring young men of the company was selected, for it took a lot of nerve to frame and propose a toast to so unpopular a man as Miser Brown. But the young man rose, and Brown, who had been notified of what was to occur, fixed his face in the customary manner of a man about to be toasted. And this was what was heard by every one except Brown, who never heard anything that was not roared into his ear:

"'Here's to you, Miser Brown. You are no better than a tramp, and it is suspected that you got most of your money dishonestly. We trust that you may get your just deserts yet, and land in the penitentiary.'

"Visible evidences of applause made Brown smile with gratification. He got upon his feet, raised his glass to his lips, and said: 'The same to you, sir.'"

General Horace Porter is another of the men whose stories always fit. It is said that he accepted the post of American Ambassador to France for the sole purpose of taking a rest from making after-dinner speeches. He can even use a pun in a manner to compel admiration, in which respect he differs from almost every one. On one occasion he said:

"New England speakers have said that the Puritans were always missionaries among the people with whom they came in contact. I saw recently a newspaper paragraph that indicated the disposition of the Puritan to busy himself with the great hereafter, and to get as close to it as possible. The paragraph announced that the *Puritan* had collided in Hell Gate. (The Puritan last-named was a steamboat.)

"But when the wooden Puritan—the New Englander, gets a man on the perilous edge, so that one or other must topple over into the pit, he takes care that he shall not be the unfortunate. He is as cautious in this respect as was the night-cab driver in front of a house where there had been a bibulous dinner party. A man emerged from the house, staggered across the sidewalk, laying out more zigzags than did our patriot sires at the siege of Yorktown, opened the door of the cab and threw himself on the seat.

"Where will I go, Sor?"

"The driver asked: 'Where will I go, sor?'

"'To hell!' was the unexpected reply.

"The cabby drove about for some moments to take a think, for though he had heard of many sure roads to the torrid destination mentioned he was not 'up' on the conveniences at the entrance, and he didn't want to scorch the paint on his cab. Soon he asked again: 'Where am I to take you, sor?'

"'To hell,' was again the reply. Cabby scratched his head, studied the situation, and asked: 'Beg pardon, sor, but can I back up when I land you?'"

To an interviewer who expected to get a good article on the difference between the English Parliament and our Congress (this was at a time when many Congressmen were tobacco-chewers) he said:

"In Parliament the men sit with their hats on and cough; in Congress they sit with their hats off and spit."

X
JOURNALISTS AND AUTHORS

Not All Journalists are Critics, nor are All Critics Fault-finders.—The Most Savage Newspapers not the Most Influential.—The Critic's Duty.—Horace Greeley.—Mark Twain's First Earnings.—A Great Publisher "Approached" by Green Goods Men.—Henry Watterson.—Opie Reid.—Quimby of the *Free Press*.—Laurence Hutton, Edwin Booth and I in Danger Together.

When you say "journalist" to a man of my profession—or of any other that devotes its time and wits to the task of amusing and entertaining people, it is taken for granted that you mean "critic," and that "critic" in turn means faultfinder. This is extremely unfair to journalists in general and to critics in particular, for not all journalists are critics, nor all critics faultfinders. Run over the names of all the critics you've heard of here or in London or Paris—critics, dramatic, musical and literary, and you will discover, to your surprise, that those who are best known and have most influence, are those who are quickest to praise and slowest to find fault.

"Trying it on the dog" is the name for this sort of thing—

As a proof of it, and how it strikes the men and women most concerned, both in pocket and pride, is the following:—almost every new play, concert and entertainment of any kind tries to give its first real performance in New York. It may endeavor to get some money out of the later rehearsals by giving a few performances out of town:—"Trying it on the dog" is the name for this sort of thing, but New York is trusted to set the pace, and this is what follows;—on the day on which New York newspapers containing a report of the performance reaches any city or town where the same attraction has been booked conditionally, or where managers or entertainment committees have heard enough in advance about it to want to hear more, there is a run on news-stands for certain New York papers. I won't indicate them closer than to say that they are not those sheets which support the brilliant chaps who skilfully ride hobbies of their own, or who are most skilled at vivisecting and eviscerating a playwright and splitting each particular hair of an actor, singer or entertainer. The papers for which there is general demand are those which tell whether the performance was good of its kind, specify the kind and tell how the audience regarded it. At the end of the third act of a new play in New York a noted critic was buttonholed in the lobby by a club-man who had a friend in the cast and asked for his opinion.

"It's a success—a great success," was the reply.

"Good! I'm so glad you like it."

"Like it? My dear fellow, I never was worse bored in my life. I'd rather have heard 'Julius Cæsar' done by a lot of high school boys. But that has nothing to do with it. If pieces were written and played for me and my kind, they'd have to charge ten dollars a ticket to get money enough to pay for the gas and music. Plays are made for audiences; this audience likes this play—likes it immensely, so other audiences will like it too, and if I don't say so in our newspaper to-morrow morning I deserve to be bounced and have this week's salary docked."

Of course it is a critic's business to see defects and call attention to them. When he does so he confers a favor upon the performer, who generally is so absorbed in what he is doing that he doesn't know what he is leaving undone or doing badly. But the faults of stage or platform can't be remedied with a sledge-hammer or a double bladed dagger—not ever if you give the dagger a turn or two after you have jabbed it in. A prominent critic said to me:

"I don't criticise a play according to my own feelings and tastes. Although I've a very good opinion of my own personal standard of judgment, I don't believe the people collectively would give a snap of the finger for it. I simply try to ascertain the opinion of the audience and express it for the benefit of the people of whom audiences are made. I greatly dislike and (mentioning a popular actor and actress) but who cares? It would not be fair to try to impress my dislikes upon others, unless I chance upon some one who takes the stage seriously, and there are only two classes who do this—conceited critics, and actors who don't get their pay. Fortunately I know very few professional people; if I knew more I would become insane through trying to dissociate their personality from their work. It is bad to know too much about anybody or anything, if you don't want to throw the world out of joint. Except in matters of morals and manners, 'where ignorance is bliss 'tis folly to be wise.' Did you ever hear how Horace Greeley once got cold feet? A friend—one of the wise, observant, upsetting kind of friends called on Greeley, one cold winter day, and found the great journalist with a favorite book in his hand, a beatific smile on his face and his feet over the register. The visitor had previously been through the building and learned that the furnace had gone wrong and been removed, the cold air flue could not be closed, and zero air was coming through all the registers, so he said:

"'Mr. Greeley, why do you keep your feet there? There is no heat—only cold air is coming up!'

"Greeley tumbled out of his chair and in the childish whine that always came to him when he was excited, replied,

"'Why didn't you let me alone? I was entirely comfortable; but now, I'm near you, I'm frozen.'"

Mention of Greeley, who was too busy a man to think of being a humorist, yet was one in spite of himself, recalls one of Mr. Depew's stories about him. A man who was in search of financial aid for some evangelistic work got into Mr. Greeley's sanctum one day, and found the great editor writing, with his head held sideways and close to the desk, like a schoolboy, as was his custom. He waved his hand, to signify that the man should go away, but Greeley had the reputation of being an easy-mark, financially, and the visitor's mind was fixed on business, so he asked,

"Mr. Greeley, how much will you give to prevent your fellow men from going to hell?"

The brilliant chaps who ride hobbies of their own—

"Not a damn cent!" was the reply, as the great editor went on writing. "Not enough of them go there now. I could name hundreds who ought to have been there long ago———" all this in a whining drawl that carried conviction with it.

Speaking of drawls, I wish all my readers could have heard Mark Twain's voice as he told me a tale of juvenile woe. I had asked him if he could remember the first money he had ever earned.

"Yes," he said. "It was at school. All boys had the habit of going to school in those days, and they hadn't any more respect for the desks than they had for the teachers. There was a rule in our school that any boy marring his desk, either with pencil or knife, would be chastised publicly before the whole school or pay a fine of five dollars. Besides the rule there was a ruler; I knew it because I had felt it; it was a darned hard one, too.

"One day I had to tell my father that I had broken the rule, and had to pay a fine or take a public whipping, and he said:

"'Sam, it would be too bad to have the name of Clemens disgraced before the whole school, so I'll pay the fine. But I don't want you to lose anything, so come up-stairs.' I went up-stairs with father and he was for-*giving* me. I came down-stairs with the feeling in one hand and the five dollars in the other, and decided that as I'd been punished once, and got used to it, I wouldn't mind taking the other licking at school. So I did, and I kept the five dollars. That was the first money I ever earned."

This unexpected shift of the moral point of view is peculiar to boys. James Whitcomb Riley, author of no end of things, humorous and pathetic, told me of a small boy who astonished his mother one night by saying his prayers in German. When reproved, he said:

"Oh, that was a joke."

"You must not joke with heaven," said his mother severely.

"Oh, the joke isn't on heaven; it's on you," was the reply.

Another small friend of Mr. Riley jumped quickly into bed one cold night. His mother said:

"Johnny, haven't you forgotten something?"

"No, mamma," was the reply. "I've made up my mind not to say my prayers to-night or to-morrow night or the night after, and then if I have luck I won't say them any more at all."

My friend Frank Doubleday, a member of a publishing firm that all authors regard admiringly, would rather get a laugh on some one than get a record-breaking novel. He is a fine, tall, handsome fellow and like many another handsome man who is really manly, he is careless of his dress, looking more like a busy farmer than a successful publisher. Going through Greenwich Street one day, near the ferries and steamboat landings, his rural appearance and manner attracted the attention of one of the "bunco" or "green goods" gentry, who accosted him with:

"Why, Mr. Brown, I'm very glad to see you."

"But my name isn't Brown," said Doubleday, in his most innocent manner.

"What? Aren't you Mr. Brown, of Paterson?"

"No, my name is Marshall P. Wilder."

"Oh, you go to hll!" growled the bunco-man with a glare.

To get back to journalists, with whom I began, I believe I have said elsewhere that Henry Watterson is the most quoted editor in the United States. Yet a lot of his best things do not appear over his signature; he says so many that only a phonograph could keep tally of them. One evening at the Riggs House in Washington he found his friend Col. Dick Wintersmith, the poet lobbyist, in a gastronomic quandary, for the colonel longed for a dinner of beefsteak and onions but dreaded to carry the perfume of onions in his breath. Watterson said:

"Colonel Dick, I'll tell you how to avoid it."

"Do!"

"Why, go to John Chamberlin's for your beefsteak and onions; when you get your bill it will take your breath entirely away."

Opie Reid, editor and author, frequently appears on the platform, to the delight of every one who listens to him. One night he was greatly puzzled, for although his audience laughed heartily no one applauded. He learned afterward that he had been engaged to entertain the inmates of a home for disabled railway employees, and his audience was composed of switchmen, each of whom had lost an arm, perhaps two. He got a laugh even on one of the dreadful eating-houses peculiar to southern railroad stations. Most of his fellow passengers were commercial travelers, and knew by experience what to expect at such places, so they got off of the train with sullen looks, as if sorry rather than glad that they were to dine, and their complainings began before they reached the table. A negro was walking to and fro on the station platform ringing a dinner-bell, and near him was a small dog howling so piteously that the darky stopped and exclaimed:

"What's you hollerin' for? *You* don't have to eat here."

My friend Quimby of the Detroit *Free Press* tells of "meeting up" with two strangers who became so friendly that soon the three were introducing themselves.

"I'm from Detroit," said Quimby to one. "Where are you from?"

"Boston," was the reply. The Bostonian turned enquiringly to the third, who said:

"I'm from Pawtucket. Now, dmn you, laugh!"

I am indebted to hundreds of critics and other journalists for kind things they have printed about me. As to authors, one of them saved my life a few years ago, and this is how it occurred:—I had rooms in Thirty-fourth Street, in New York, next door to the late Laurence Hutton, author of many well-known books. One night, on returning home very late, I discovered that I had neglected to take my keys, so I was practically locked out. I rang the bell, but no one responded. Suddenly I noted that lights were still burning in Mr. Hutton's house, and I recalled that he had given a dinner that night to Mr. Edwin Booth, the tragedian. Hutton was the most obliging neighbor any one could have had, so I rang him up, told him of my trouble, and asked permission to go into his yard and climb the division fence, after which I would get into my own house through a rear window.

"All right, Marshall," Hutton replied, "and I'll go with you, and help you over the fence."

My only fear was of a lodger in my own house—a nervous man, apprehensive of burglars, and who kept revolvers and a quick temper ready for use at any moment he might be aroused. I said as much to Mr. Hutton, and the affair immediately changed from a neighborly courtesy to an adventure with a spice of danger to make it more attractive. Mr. Booth who had overheard the conversation, announced that he wasn't to be left out of any fun in sight, so we three crept silently into Hutton's back yard like three burglars, or more like three schoolboys out for mischief. Finding that he could not lift me over, as he had intended, Hutton got a chair, stood upon it and helped me to the top of the fence, which was high. Even there I was no better off, for the fence was as tall as I was not, so like Mohammed's coffin I was poised between heaven and earth and unable to drop without breaking something. But Hutton was a man of expedients: he stood on the extreme top of the chair-back, leaned over the fence and held my cane, by its crook, as if it were a dangling rope, down which I slid safely, thanks to a running fire of tragic stage-whispers, by Mr. Booth, to the general effect, that it is always well to keep very tight hold of a good thing, until you strike a better one.

I reached the ground safely and began the more dangerous part of my enterprise, which was to open a window of the main floor without rousing the lodger who was a light sleeper and kept pistols. A spectator, had there been any excepting the blasé man in the moon, might have gazed at an unusual scene—honest little me apparently burglarizing a house, while a prominent author and the greatest living tragedian, both honorable and law-abiding citizens, standing shakily on the highest back-bar of a single chair, steadying themselves by leaning heavily on a fence-top and giving me all the moral support that could be signified by heart-throbs and irregular breathings. Suddenly Hutton whispered hoarsely,

"Look out, Marshall!"

But I looked up, and right into the business end of a revolver, and I did not at all approve of what I saw. Had I looked toward the fence I would have beheld two eminent Americans in the undignified act of "ducking." But I was too busily engaged in flattening myself against the window to have eyes for anything but fragmentary visions of the world to come: I shriveled so utterly that it seemed a million years before I had lungs enough to shout.

"Don't shoot! It's Marshall!"

We never settled it to our mutual satisfaction—Hutton's, and Booth's and mine, by which of us the world might have lost most had the revolver been fired and hit one of us. Mr. Booth was the incarnation of modesty, Hutton could eloquently praise any one but himself, while I—— But, as already said, we never agreed as to which would have been the world's greatest loss.

XI
THE UNEXPECTED

Robert Hilliard and I and a Dog.—Hartford's Actors and Playwrights.—A Fit that Caused a Misfit.—A Large Price to Hear a Small Man.—Jim Corbett and I.—A Startled Audience.—Captain Williams and "Red" Leary.—"Joe" Choate to the Rescue.—Bait for a Dude.—Deadheads.—Within an Inch of Davy Jones.—Perugini and Four Fair Adorers.—Scanlon and Kernell.

In one respect personal experiences are like jokes—those least expected cause the most lasting impression. I may be excused, therefore, for recording some of both.

Some years ago a party of ladies and gentlemen, among whom were Mr. Hilliard and myself visited David's Island, an important military post on Long Island Sound. We were handsomely entertained during the day, so at night we endeavored to return the compliment. There was a large gathering in the mess room, the post band gave a few selections and Mr. Hilliard announced that he would recite "Christmas Night in the Workhouse." Instantly a large Newfoundland dog who had been quite conspicuous, looked sad, dropped upon the floor and went to sleep. The joke was on Bob and every one was obliged to laugh. But when my turn came and I announced a few stories about camp life that dog arose, looked straight and reproachfully into my eyes and walked out of the door. When the laughter subsided I felt obliged to say:

"I don't blame you, old chap."

As I was a Hartford boy, I have always had a special liking for the men and women whom that city has given to the stage and platform. They make an imposing array, too—William Gillette, Mark Twain, Otis Skinner, Harry Woodruff, Lew Dockstader, Francis Carlyle, Musical Dale, Frank Lawton, C. B. Dillingham and Mesdames Lucille Saunders and Emma Eames.

I greatly admire Mr. Gillette's plays; they contain so wonderful a variety of characters that it seems to me he must have searched the whole country for originals. One day he told me of a pleasant trip he had made on the St. Lawrence River and said:

"I'm going to live up there."

"Are you? Where?" I asked, supposing he would name a hotel where a large lot of human nature could be studied, but he named a lonely part of the Thousand Islands, and said he owned an island there, so I asked:

"Why do you go there? You will be all alone."

"I want to be alone," he replied.

"Will no one live there but yourself?"

"No one but a hen—a little bantam hen."

"What do you mean by that? What do you want of a hen?"

"Well, I've always had great fondness and respect for hens, but have been unable to get acquainted with them, but this is my chance."

Mark Twain was once asked to write a testimonial for a map of the world, and this is what he wrote:

"Before using your wonderful map, my family were afflicted with fits, but since using it they have nothing but freckles."

There was a time when I wished for Mark's wonderful map, for I was afflicted by a fit. It was at an entertainment at Long Branch given in aid of the Monmouth Hospital. Many actors and actresses who were stopping at "the Branch" gave their services, among them Neil Burgess, Mr. and Mrs. Oliver Dowd Byron, Mr. and Mrs. Matt Snyder, Mr. and Mrs. Frank Chanfrau, Miss Maggie Mitchell, Miss Theresa Vaughn and others. I was to appear, and when I arrived, I saw Miss Vaughn and Mr. Snyder, who was stage manager, holding an animated discussion. Snyder came over to me and said:

"Miss Vaughn has been billed to follow you, but she doesn't wish to. She would like to precede you."

"All right," I replied, "I'm perfectly willing."

She went out and made a great hit. Then my turn came, and I had just got a recitation under way when a woman in the audience began to have a fit, at the most critical part of my number. I had to stop as it was not a duet, and go off of the stage. Mr. Snyder asked:

"What's the matter, Marsh?"

"There's a woman out there having a fit."

"Oh, go back and do the best you can," he replied.

"This is not where I fit," I answered. But I went back and told my pianist to play number seven of my repertoire, which was called "Poor Thing!"

The audience saw the joke, and helped me out, but I wish my readers could have been in my position if they do not believe that fit was an affliction—one which Miss Vaughn was fortunate enough to escape.

A great many men have told me they greatly wanted to hear me recite, and I am convinced that one in particular meant what he said. I refer to Bingham the ventriloquist. He chanced to be in a town where I was to appear before the Young Men's Christian Association. He went to the hall to reserve a good seat, but was told that no tickets would be sold; the entertainment would be for members only.

"But I want to hear Mr. Wilder," he said, "and this is my only chance within sight. Is there no way of my getting in?"

"None: unless you join the Association."

Incredible though it may seem, Bingham did join the Y. M. C. A. for the sole purpose of listening to me. He never asked me to refund his initiation fee on the ground that he didn't get the worth of it, either, though I've scrupulously avoided recalling the incident to his memory.

"There's James J. Corbett!" "Which One?"

Nothing is more unexpected by any one than to be mistaken for some one else. One day while I was walking with James J. Corbett, the handsome actor-pugilist, who is about twice as tall as I, two young ladies passed us and one exclaimed:

"Why, there's James J. Corbett."

"Which one?" the other asked.

Light-weight though I am, there was a time when I got Corbett badly rattled. He was living at Asbury Park, training for one of his fights, and I, while in a railway car with him, got out some friends—a pack of cards—and did some tricks for Jim. Soon I got him so puzzled that he exclaimed:

"Hold on there, Marsh! These tricks get me nutty."

It was the unexpected that brought James Young, the actor, a roar of laughter one evening when he addressed as follows an audience composed entirely of his own acquaintances:

"My friends—I cannot call you ladies and gentlemen, for I know you all."

It was the unexpected, too, that only severely jarred Capt. Alex. Williams, a noted ex-police official in New York. A woman fainted in the street, the captain caught her by one arm, and "Red" Leary, a noted criminal by the other.

"Cap'n," said "Red" politely, "this is the first time you and me have 'worked' together."

Minister Choate—"Joe" Choate, has a reserve fund of the unexpected. Some American dishes were served up at a breakfast party in England, one being ham and eggs. A young lady at the minister's right was ignorant of the slippery ways of fried eggs on a dish, so she accidentally spilled the contents of her plate.

"Oh, Mr. Choate!" she exclaimed, "I don't know what to do, for I've dropped an egg on the floor," and Choate replied:

"If I were you, I'd cackle."

"Ignorant of the Slippery Ways of Fried Eggs."

Matt Snyder, the actor, found at his table one night a young man so elaborately dressed as to be a startling dude, so he asked his daughter:

"What did you bait your hook with to catch that?" but he was floored by the sweet reply:

"Cake, papa."

Sometimes the unexpected will cause a man to be grievously wounded in the house of his friends. Here is an illustration, clipped from a New York newspaper:

"Marshall P. Wilder, the professional humorist, was in the Lambs' Club, surrounded by some spirits, yesterday evening. He looked at his watch and remarked wearily, 'I've got to run away, for I've got to go up-town to be funny. It's an awful bore.'

"Wilton Lackaye, who has been taking up the rôle of smart cynicism left by poor Maurice Barrymore, drawled, in his most irritating manner: 'I wouldn't do it, then. Why don't you give your usual entertainment?'

"'Cruel boy,' chirped Wilder, as he made for the door."

Lackaye is also the man who gravely suggested to a patriotic Scotchman that the reason the bagpipes were put in the rear of a regiment in battle was that the men would be so anxious to get away from the music that they would run toward the enemy.

One of the greatest nuisances of the entertainment business, the theatre and all other "shows," is the persistent "deadhead." Every good fellow in the profession likes so much to have his friends see his performance that he provides free tickets to the extent of his ability, often paying cash for them. But people who are not friends—some who are not even acquaintances, are the most determined deadheads; to have heard about their deceased mother-in-law is reason enough—to them, for a demand for a free ticket. Yet a man on the stage or platform is sometimes startled by seeing close personal friends in the line, cash in hand, at the box-office, and is reminded of the story Senator Jones of Nevada tells about crossing a river out west. He reached the ferry but no boat was there. He saw a man across the stream chopping wood, so he shouted, "Hello, there! Where's the boat?"

The Passengers Consisted of Three Men and a Half.

"No boat, wade across," was the man's answer, "and I will direct you. Walk ten feet to the right,—five feet to the left. Look out—there's a do big hole there! Now three feet to the right." Arriving on the other side of the stream, the senator asked, "What shall I pay you?"

"Wa-all," said the man, "there's been a dozen men across this ferry, and you are the first that ever offered to pay anything, so I guess I'll let you dead-head it."

Occasionally the unexpected is delightful in the extreme.

Before Charles Frohman became the busiest man and Napoleon of the dramatic stage, he used to affiliate frequently with the Lambs' Club, of which he was a member. One day the Lambs gave what they call their "washing," otherwise their summer treat or picnic, at an island in the sound owned by Lester Wallack. At high tide boats could land passengers on the island, and in the morning the Lambs were safely landed. But at night the steamer which brought us was anchored out about a half mile from the shore. When the entertainment was at an end, the members had to be rowed in small boats to the steamer. The oarsman of the boat I was in was a large, corpulent chap. The passengers consisted of Charles Frohman, also a heavy weight, George Fawcett and myself, making three men and a half. This weighed the boat down to almost within an inch of the water, and coupled with the fact that neither Mr. Frohman, Mr. Fawcett nor myself could swim, I fully expected it would be our last sail, but we reached the steamer in safety. One little false move on the part of either of us would have caused the head of the Dramatic Syndicate, an excellent actor and "Merrily Yours" to be busy—for a moment or two, in "Davy Jones's Locker."

Augustus Pitou tells a suggestive story of the unexpected. Late at night he asked for a barber at a hotel. It was "after hours," but after much delay one appeared and asked as a favor of Mr. Pitou if he would kindly lie on the lounge and let him shave him in a horizontal position. Mr. Pitou consented. The touch was so gentle he fell asleep. When he awoke and felt of his chin he said:

"That's the gentlest shave I have ever had."

"Well, sir, you are the first live man I have ever shaved."

The man was an undertaker's barber!

Nat Goodwin tells how Billy Mannering, a brilliant old time negro comedian, sprang the unexpected on a hotel proprietor. The company was having hard luck on one night stands. Country hotels were as bad in those days as now—even worse. The boys were eating breakfast one morning when Bill came down late and said:

"Boys, how is it? About the same as all the rest of the hotels?"

"Yes, Billy."

In came the proprietor and said: "Good-morning, gentlemen."

Billy asked: "Who are you?"

"I'm the proprietor, sir."

"So you're the proprietor! Do you know you are a brave man? If I were you, I would live out in the woods, and not come near the hotel. I would be afraid to face my boarders."

"How's that? Are not the beds all right?"

"Yes, but we can't eat our beds. Still, you have two things here that can't be improved on."

"What are they?" asked the proprietor, filling out his chest.

"Why, your pepper and salt."

I played the unexpected on several people aboard a certain ocean steamship, on which my friend Perugini was a passenger. Several of the ladies on board became enamored of "Handsome Jack," and were very anxious to be introduced to him. They made me their confidant, but Perry was not much of a "masher" and did not care to meet them. At this time, he had an affliction of which I am glad to say he has been cured; he was deaf. One morning I rapped on his stateroom door, and getting no response, I concluded I would run the risk and go in. There he lay, sound asleep. His valet had preceded me, and everything looked as neat and cozy as could be. Perry did not hear me, no matter what noise I made. I went on deck, found four of the young ladies and said:

"Now's your chance to meet Perugini; just follow me." They accompanied me and all four looked in at the door, but were afraid to go in.

"Oh, don't he look lovely," said one.

"Isn't he charming—I could just hug him!" said another. I went in; as he did not hear me they took courage and one by one they stole in and got near to Perugini. I slipped toward the door and quickly closed it. The girls were too frightened even to cry out. Then I took hold of Jack and gave him a shake that awakened him. Poor Jack! He was more frightened than the four girls put together. All I got out of him when he and I got on deck was,

"Oh, Marsh! How could you?"

Kyrle Bellew was a passenger on the same steamer. My acquaintance with Mr. Bellew is a most pleasant one, so I know he will forgive me if I detail this little joke, which, like all my jokes, was played in good nature.

On the ship he wore a yachting cap and a full yachting costume, including a big cord around his neck, to which was attached a telescope. In the evening he would walk up to the side of the steamer, pull out this glass full-length, gaze out on the ocean at some distant ship, close it and again walk down the deck, posing in an effective manner, seemingly unconscious of the amusement he afforded the other passengers. In a burlesque spirit I arranged, as best I could, an imitation of him. I got a seaman's trousers, blouse and hat, and extemporized a sort of wig as like to my friend's as possible; to a piece of rope about my neck I attached a Belfast beer bottle. At a safe distance I walked up and down the deck and gave the passengers the benefit of my burlesque. I don't believe Bellew ever saw me. If he had, I fear it would have been my finish; still, I think he would have enjoyed the practical joke afterward.

Even a book-canvasser can be floored by the unexpected. James Whitcomb Riley tells of an insinuating member of this profession who rang the bell of a handsome residence and when a specially aggressive looking servant opened the door he asked politely:

"Is the lady in?"

"What do ye mane?" the girl asked. "I'd have ye know we're all ladies in this house!"

In another part of this book I have referred to entertainments I gave at an insane asylum—a place where the unexpected should be the rule, to the performer. But at the Bloomingdale Asylum I once saw it work the other way, and to an extent that was pathetic all round. Among the inmates were Scanlon and Kernell—two men who had thousands of times delighted great audiences with song and joke. I knew of their presence but how they would look or feel I had no means of imagining.

One of my assistants for the occasion was Miss Cynthia Rogers of Toledo, Ohio. The programme was not printed, nor arranged in detail, so we were in ignorance as to what songs had been selected. Miss Rogers "went on" dressed as an Irish lad, beginning in a copy of Scanlon's familiar make-up, the most popular song of his own composition, "Mollie O."

Everybody looked at Scanlon. His face was suddenly aglow with interest. His lips followed, word by word, the course of the melody. He raised one hand and motioned as if he were directing the music. At the close of the first verse, when the building shook with applause, he smiled happily. He was living his triumphs over at that minute, oblivious to his surroundings. He was impatient for the next verse; he followed the words intently; his face was flushed, the old inspiration showed in his eyes, and when the applause broke forth again he laughed and bowed his head.

"Did you see that man?" Miss Rogers asked me a second later. "Did you ever see such an expression? Who is he—that young man yonder, with his head bowed?"

"Why, I thought you must have known," I replied. "That's Scanlon."

"Scanlon the actor?"

"Yes. The author of your song."

Miss Rogers was tearfully uncertain, as she went on to respond to an encore, whether she had done right or wrong. She sang "In It" and the "Latch Key in the Door." Then Scanlon was brought back to us and Miss Rogers was introduced to him.

"I want to thank you," he said simply. "I felt as I used to, you know. Some day I will sing it again. You are very pretty and you sing well."

If there was one man in the audience blind to the pathos of the scene which had just occurred it was Harry Kernell, the comedian. He had looked on quietly, his face impassive, his hands clasped loosely over one knee. He smiled when Scanlon came back to the seat just in front of him; then his face became fixed and vacant as before.

Kernell raised his face again as his wife who had been sitting beside him, left her seat. He seemed to have forgotten her, and to be hearing nothing and seeing nothing, when I announced the next number on the programme.

"We have a pleasant surprise for you," I said, smiling in anticipation. "Mrs. Kernell is here; she came up to see her husband, my old friend, and we wouldn't let her refuse to sing for you."

But Kernell did not look up until his wife, Queenie Vassar, began singing. The little woman watched him tenderly. The poor fellow understood. After that, no lover could have been more appreciative than he was. It was the one voice in all the world that could move him. Scanlon turned and whispered to him, but Kernell's soul was in the song. Quickly he looked ten years younger than he does ordinarily. He seemed grateful for the applause, and eager for another song, and another, so Mrs. Kernell sang "Peggy Cline," "Sligo" and "The Bowery."

After that Kernell sat still and gloomy. The spell was broken that had made him young. The deep lines came back on his face, his shoulders stooped and he was an old man again, listless and helpless. One could hardly imagine him the man that scattered sunshine so royally, laughing his way to fame, building his triumphs on the happiness he gave to others.

Miss Claude Rogers played a mandolin solo of her own composing with "Il Trovatore" for an encore. Later she played again, and was encored repeatedly. As for me, I had as difficult an audience as ever confronted a humorist, or any other sort of speaker, but the success was complete and the fun was contagious. It was curious to see how an audience, of so many different states of mind, could be affected by humor and music. I have had far less appreciative audiences among sane people, and have been at my wits' end to rouse them. Here is a story that tells how Digby Bell once roused a cold audience without giving offense; it proved the biggest hit of his act. He recently had to deal with a particularly frigid audience, and the best of his jokes met with but indifferent success. There happened to be a little flag fastened on one side of the stage, and the humorist, after delivering his last joke ineffectually, ran over, gravely pulled the banner down to half-mast and made his exit. The audience appreciated the sarcastic proceeding, and applauded him till he was obliged to give them a little additional entertainment, and this time he had no need to complain of their appreciation.

XII
SUNSHINE IN SHADY PLACES

On Blackwell's Island.—Snakes and Snake Charmers.—Insane People as Audiences.—A Poorhouse That was a Large House.—I am Well Known by Another Profession.—Criminals are not Fools.—Some Pathetic Experiences.—The Largest Fee I Ever Received.

For many years the late Cornelius Vanderbilt paid me a regular salary to visit a lot of charitable institutions,—the Almshouse, the Penitentiary, the Newsboys' Lodging House and a number of other places, where laughter was not part of the regular daily exercises and was therefore valued most highly. One of the places frequently visited was the Insane Asylum on Blackwell's Island, and I was often invited to lunch with the Superintendent. A harmless patient, who was employed as waiter, was at times quite amusing through her faculty for seeing people where none existed. She would often stop and argue indignantly with some one whom she imagined was in her way, and to see how with a tray of dishes in her hands she scolded the empty air, was first very funny and afterward creepingly uncanny. Once she imagined that one of these annoying people had climbed upon the table, and she attacked him so savagely with a broom that we had to have a new set of dishes and goblets.

One night a severe storm compelled me to remain at the Asylum. My friend the house-surgeon gave me a comfortable room, near the wing where the more violent patients were confined. In the middle of the night, one of these began to rave and scream; his appeals for help were pitiful. I put my head out of my door and asked an attendant what was the matter.

"For God's Sake Come! There's a Woman in my Room."

"He's seeing snakes," was the reply, "but he'll be all right in a few minutes." Just then the man informed the neighborhood of a new misfortune, by shouting,

"For God's sake come to me quick. There's a woman in my room!" Again he became quiet and the attendant said,

"It's all right now."

"Yes," I replied: "she must have been a snake charmer."

I always found insane audiences very appreciative. Probably the majority of them were "out of their head" on one subject only. Certainly their enjoyment of song and pantomime was very keen, and their interest in my exhibitions of ventriloquism was quite pathetic. Whenever I threw my voice in a certain direction, some of them would look under chairs and tables, in search of the supposed person who was talking. The poor creatures took such hold of my sympathies that I exerted myself to amuse them optically, for the eye is the surest route to the wits. I would, while on the platform, make quickly different articles of colored paper and give them to the patients, whose pleasure was as childlike as it was sincere.

On one of my visits I was startled by coming face to face with a notice which read "Almshouse wagon reserved for Marshall P. Wilder and party from 12 to 4." On inquiry I learned that this wagon was a Pooh Bah among vehicles, serving by turns as patrol wagon, ambulance and hearse, so it took some jollying of myself to ward off gruesome imaginings and keep my risibilities in working order.

At one of the Almshouse entertainments at which the room was packed, I said, "This is the first time I ever knew a poor house to be such a large house," and the audience "caught on" as quick as a flash.

The only painful experience of my years as an entertainer among the public institutions was at the Home for Consumptives, at Fordham. The patients were cheerful and spirited, as consumptives always are, and they seemed to enjoy my jokes mightily, but laughter usually brought on violent fits of coughing, so I would have to wait from five to ten minutes after a joke, before I dared venture another.

I always recall with pleasure a visit to Elmira, where I had the brightest and most responsive audience of my whole career. It was at the State Reformatory, and there were three or four thousand prisoners in the audience. Mr. Brockway, the Superintendent, said he would like me to talk about ten minutes, and asked kindly if that would be too long to talk continuously. Before I appeared he said to the boys,

"We have with us this evening Mr. Marshall P. Wilder. How many of you know him?"

Fully three-quarters of that great assemblage raised their hands. It was quite flattering to be so well known in a "profession" as cautious and exclusive as theirs. I found my audience so quick, appreciative and responsive that instead of restricting myself to ten minutes, I learned afterward that I had talked an hour and thirty-five minutes!

Laughter was not Part of the Daily Exercises.

It may be argued by some skeptics that these boys and young men, being prisoners, were grateful for any entertainment that would break the monotony of their daily routine, but I prefer to believe their appreciation was due entirely to their native cleverness. It takes brains to place and accomplish anything, whether legal or illegal, and prisoners of the class that is sent to the Reformatory have proved their ability to think, or they would not be there. There are thousands of clever men who are good, and of good men who are stupid, but among criminals the rule is not reversible, for I have yet to see a criminal who is a fool.

I met many interesting and pathetic personalities while engaged in the institutions. One old man in the Home for Incurables was so badly paralyzed, that he could move only his hands, and these but a few inches. He would lie all day on his back, with his hands on his chest, holding a little switch broken from a peach-tree, with which he would gently scratch his face and head. This was his only occupation and pleasure; it was also the limit of his ability to move. Yet this pitiable old man was always smiling and happy; he would have repelled the idea that he was unfortunate, for he was constantly recounting his blessings and comforts—his bed, his food, his kindly attention, and not the least of all, his little peach-twig.

Another interesting case in the same Home was a feeble minded boy—almost an imbecile. His physical development was perfect; he was healthy and very strong, yet his vacant eyes, dropped jaw and frontal expression of head indicated plainly a sad lack of wits. He was gentle and tractable and devoted to the matron, who by demonstration had taught him how to be useful in many ways. His strength was utilized in moving helpless patients from bed to chairs, or vice versa, and he had been taught to change the beds and do other work in the men's ward as neatly as a woman.

It Takes Brains to Accomplish Anything.

But his chief duty, and one at which he excelled, was to act as baker for the institution. The matron had taught him, and he had followed her method so faithfully that every day he dropped a little flour on the floor and then wiped it up; the matron had chanced to this "aside" in the first lesson, so it was impossible to convince the boy that this was not a necessary detail of bread-making. His bread was delicious too; he made thirty-six loaves every day in a triple oven holding three pans of twelve loaves each, and never had a failure. Being exact in every way, his success was always assured.

One old woman, who might have been admitted to this admirable home, refused to enter it; she said she preferred the Almshouse. She had been wealthy in her youth but, through unbridled extravagance, had been reduced to poverty so dire, that for years she had eked out a miserable existence by selling newspapers. When she became too ill and feeble to do even this, it was suggested that she should enter the Home for Incurables, but she refused, saying that she would go to no private institution, but to the poorhouse, which, when she was rich, she had helped to maintain. A charitable gentleman who would have helped her, and to whom she expressed her desire, assured her that she should have her choice in the matter, foolish though it was. She asked him if instead of being conveyed in the almshouse wagon, she might be moved in some other way; her would-be benefactor assured her she should go in his own carriage, and he himself would be her escort. He invited me to accompany them, I having already met the old woman and been interested in her. At the appointed time we called for her and as she stepped into the carriage she was visibly elated by the thought of once more going through the streets in a manner like that of her wealthy days. She had dressed for the occasion in style truly wonderful. Her bonnet, though of startling construction, commanded attention by its antiquity; a rag of a camel's hair shawl was pinned tightly across her narrow chest; a black silk reticule hung from one thin arm, which was encased in a long suede glove, boasting the special advantage of leaving her fingers free while her other hand was covered with a lace mitt of antique fashion.

She had Dressed in a Style Truly Wonderful.

During the drive she sat stiffly erect, gazed with scorn at people who were merely walking, and occasionally dropped a stiff, formal speech, after the manner of polite conversation in her youthful days. When we had almost reached our destination, she said to my friend her escort:

"For your extreme kindness to me, I should like to bestow upon you a slight remembrance, something saved from the beautiful things I once owned." She put her hand into her reticule and we expected to see a trinket such as women prize, but she pulled out a pistol and apparently leveled it at my friend. We gasped, instantly convinced that she had lost the tiny bit of sanity that was left to her, but in a second we saw that she was presenting it to, not at, him. It was a pretty toy with a pearl handle and inlaid with silver, but, like herself, rusty and dilapidated. It was her last bit of elegance and all the poor creature had to offer in token of her gratitude.

A touching feature of this Home was the manner of furnishing the rooms for the pay patients. When the wing for this class of inmates was built it was believed that a long time would elapse before there would be money enough in the treasury to furnish the rooms. A kind hearted woman who visited the house weekly with donations of snuff, tobacco and candy conceived a clever plan. She had just lost her mother, in whose name she presented the entire furnishings of her mother's room to the Home. Word of this got abroad; other people followed her example and in a short time the entire wing was furnished in similar manner; so now the visitor to the home sees a wing of four stories, the halls lined with doors on each of which is a brass plate engraved with the name of the person who furnished the room in memory of parent, brother, sister or child.

This is an appropriate place in my story to tell of the largest fee I ever received for entertaining, for although the giver was not heartily interested in a public institution, he was *en route* for one.

I was traveling in the West and looking about the railway car for a friend, an acquaintance or even some one with whom I might scrape acquaintance, for I don't enjoy being alone a long time, when I saw, in one end of the car, an officer with a prisoner. It did not take long to see that the prisoner was handcuffed, his feet were shackled to the bottom of the seat, and behind him were two guards with revolvers in hand. Evidently the prisoner was of some consequence, although he looked like a mere boy. He sat with bowed head and a hopeless look on his white face. His eyes, which in so young a man ought to have been bright and merry, were downcast and full of gloom.

I ventured over to the party and soon recognized one of the guards, as a man I had seen in a similar capacity at the Elmira Reformatory. In reply to my questions about the prisoner, he told me that the youth had been brought on extradition proceedings from England, after evading capture a long time. His crime had been peculiarly atrocious and he was now being taken to Kansas City for trial.

I was sorry for the officer and guards, as well as for the prisoner, for there can't be much that's cheery in hunting down and manacling a fellow man, no matter how bad he may be. Besides, they looked about as uncomfortable as the prisoner, so I got off a joke or two to brace them up. Soon the prisoner raised his head and manifested a trace of interest. Then I asked if I might try some card tricks on them. Of course I might; it's hard to find a man so troubled, that he won't forget his misery a moment or two over a card trick.

All the men in the car were soon looking on, but I kept my eye and heart on the prisoner; no matter what he deserved, it was plain to see what he needed. The poor wretch became thoroughly aroused from his dejection, so I sandwiched tricks and stories and saw him "pick up" a little more after each one. I "played at him," and him alone, as actors sometimes do at one man in a theatre audience. It was a big contract, and I was a small man, but I was bound to see it through. It took two hours of hard work, but at the end of that time the prisoner was an entirely different man in appearance. His eyes were bright, the color had come back to his cheeks, his whole manner had changed; he had forgotten his past and for the moment he was a man again. When we were near Kansas City, he asked me if I wouldn't shake hands with him, and he said that I could never know what my kindness in the past two hours had been to him. The look he gave me, as I clasped his manacled hand, was the biggest pay I ever got in my life.

XIII
"BUFFALO BILL"

He Works Hard but Jokes Harder.—He and I Stir up a Section of Paris.—In Peril of a Mob.—My Indian Friends in the Wild West Company.—Bartholdi and Cody.—English Bewilderment Over the "Wild West" People.—Major "Jack" Burke.—Cody as a Stage-driver.—Some of His Western Stories.—When He Had the Laugh on Me.

My acquaintance with Col. William F. Cody—"Buffalo Bill"—dates back to a time when I was a boy at Hartford and he was an actor in Ned Buntline's play "The Prairie Waif." His life had been strenuous in the extreme ever since he was thirteen years of age, but neither hardship nor danger had ever suppressed his inherent merriment and his longing to get a joke out of something or on somebody.

Our acquaintance was renewed at Rochester, where I had for schoolmate his only son, Kit Carson Cody, named for a famous scout of fifty years ago. The death of this boy was a great and lasting grief to his father, and his memory became more and more a link to bind the Colonel and me together, so in time we formed a close and lasting friendship. Whenever we chanced to be in the same city we were together so much that we became nicknamed "The Corsican Brothers."

When the "Wild West" Company first went to Paris I was one of Buffalo Bill's guests for several weeks. The Paris shopkeepers and theatre managers had heard of the enormous success of the "Wild West" in England and some of them, who feared it might divert money which otherwise would find its way into their pockets, arranged for a powerful "clacque" on the opening day, not to applaud but to disturb the performance and discourage Cody, so that he would leave the city. They did not know their man, so they had only their expense for their pains. Besides, even a Paris mob, which is said to be the meanest in the world, would think twice before "demonstrating" much in the face of an arena full of Indians and crack shots. The performance went on with little or no annoyance, but after it ended a great crowd burst into the ring and almost caused a riot. Suddenly another French peculiarity was manifested; a single gendarme worked his way to the centre of the crowd and fired a bullet from his pistol; in an instant the multitude dispersed. The worst of the French people respect the majesty of the law—when it is backed by firearms.

I soon duplicated, as well as I could, the Colonel's plains costume, which he always wore in the streets as an advertisement. I too appeared in buckskin trousers, fringed leggings, pistol belt and broad sombrero hat. I must have looked like an animated mushroom, but the Parisians were quick to note the resemblance and to dub me "le petit Buffalo Bill." Cody himself generally called me his "stove-in-pard."

One morning the Colonel went out to be shaved and asked me to accompany him. As both were dressed in wild west costume, to which the colonel had added a pair of pistols and a knife, a large crowd followed on and lingered about the shop we entered. A Parisian shopkeeper generally has his wife with him, to act as cashier and general manager, and the barber to whom we had gone had a chic and attractive wife, regarding whom Cody and I exchanged admiring remarks in English, at the risk of the barber understanding us and becoming disagreeable. Then Cody seated himself and asked the barber:

"Do you speak English?"

"Non, m'sieur,"—with apologetic eyebrows and shoulders. The colonel thrust his hands into his long brown curls and said:

"I want you to put a little oil on my hair and rub it in; compre?"

"Oui, oui, m'sieur."

Then Bill asked: "Marsh, what is French for shave?"

My French was as limited as his, so I replied:

"'Razoo,' I guess."

"And I want you to razoo my face, compre?"

"Oui, oui, m'sieur."

The barber shaved his customer, but he had mistaken the sign language of Cody's first order, for he raised a pair of shears to clip the Colonel's long hair—one of his most treasured possessions and features; in fact, like Samson of Biblical fame, his hair was the secret of his strength. Just as the barber lifted a lock and posed the shears for the first snip Bill saw the situation in a mirror. With a cowboy yell that would have made a Comanche Indian green with envy he sprang from the chair to save his hair. The barber, who had been working with bated breath, appalled by the savage appearance of his customer, dropped his shears and his knees shook, as, with chattering teeth, he begged for mercy. The wife's screams added to the confusion, the lingering crowd pressed in and was reinforced by a gendarme who began a rapid fire of questions in excited French. No explanations that were offered in either tongue were comprehended by the parties who spoke the other language and, as the barber seemed consumed with a desire to get rid of us, we hurried away in a cab, the barber's wife following us with a torrent of imprecations—and she so pretty, too!

One day, while the show was at Paris, we saw a distinguished looking man pressing against the rope stretched around Colonel Cody's tent. When he found opportunity he said, in excellent English:

"We hurried away."

"Pardon me, Colonel Cody, but I should like to speak to you. I have many friends in your great country—a country for which I have a sincere admiration."

"I am very glad to see you," the colonel replied wearily; he had heard this same speech so often. "May I ask your name?"

"My name is Bartholdi," modestly replied the sculptor whose magnificent statue, "Liberty Enlightening the World," has endeared him to Americans. From the moment he made himself known to Cody he "owned the show."

Indians generally manifest extreme suspicion of white men, but while I was Colonel Cody's guest I made friends of some of the chiefs and braves, especially Red Shirt and Flat Iron. The former, a famous scout and warrior, has been called "The Red Napoleon" for his knowledge of military tactics, his commanding dignity and reserve. He has a fine physique, and a noble head, while his bearing is absolutely regal. He has always been friendly to the whites, and was a valuable ally of Buffalo Bill in many raids against his unruly brethren.

I knew Red Shirt was fond of me, but no one else would have imagined it from his manner toward me, for your Indian friend does not slap you on the back or buttonhole you with a joke, after the manner of white men. Later I learned of the earnestness of his regard through a story told me by Bronco Bill, the Wild West Company's interpreter. It seems that, after Red Shirt had left the company for a few months and returned to his reservation, he found an old illustrated paper in which was a portrait he thought was mine. He could not verify it, for he was unable to read. Although the winter had set in and snow was deep on the ground he rode twenty miles to the home of Bronco Bill to ask if the face was mine. Being assured that it really was a picture of his friend, he took it back home and fastened it to the wall of his cabin—an unusual proceeding, for an Indian regards it beneath his dignity to indicate emotion, even among his own people.

When the Wild West was last at Madison Square Garden, I again met Red Shirt and Flat Iron. The former was very glad to see me, so the interpreter told me, and I had reason to believe it, but no bystander would have imagined it from his reserved manner and impassive face. Flat Iron, who is an exception to almost all Indians in having a twinkling eye and vivacious manner, rapidly asked me many questions: was I stronger?—had I a squaw?—etc. The fact that I was unmarried had worried him so greatly in the earlier days of our friendship that he offered to select me a charming squaw from among his own grandchildren.

"He offered to select me a charming squaw."

Flat Iron is a shrewd financier, with a money getting system peculiarly his own, which he had worked successfully on many whites. In New York, he sometimes walked alone, in a street full of people, muttering to himself and staring at the sky. When he saw that he had excited curiosity—and an Indian can see out of the back of his head as well as out of both sides of it, he would stop, place several nickels,—never pennies, on the sidewalk, and make solemn "passes" over them, as if doing an incantation act. Occasionally he would look aside, and indicate by signs that the observers should add to the number of nickels. These additions he would arrange in geometric figures, which always lacked some point or line. Bystanders would supply the deficiency, the coins would be rearranged, still with missing parts, and the mysterious passes would continue, accompanied by solemn gazes heavenward. This pantomime would continue until the crowd had parted with all its nickels; then suddenly the old man would pick up the entire collection, stow it in his pocket and stalk off as jauntily as a broker who has succeeded in unloading a lot of wild-cat stocks on a confiding public.

While the Wild West was at Manchester I had my hundredth laugh—perhaps it was my thousandth, at the density of intelligent Englishmen's ignorance regarding American people and ways. Colonel Cody, his partner and business manager, "Nate Salsbury," were standing together, when an Englishman approached and asked for Mr. Salsbury. Nate asked what he could do for him and the man replied:

"I'm the Greffic."

"The wha-at?"

"The Greffic—the London Greffic. I make sketches, don'cher know?"

"Oh! The London *Graphic?* All right. Sail right in. You might begin with Cody."

"And who is Cody?" the artist asked.

"Why, Cody is Buffalo Bill!"—Salsbury almost screamed, he was so amazed.

"And does he speak English?"

It may be admitted, in explanation, that some artists are as ignorant as idiots of anything but their own profession. But list to a tale of an American lady and an English clergyman who was an Oxford graduate and a great reader. He was also of charming manner and conversed brilliantly. The lady was the first American he had ever met, and he confessed to her that he was startled by her complexion, for he had supposed that all inhabitants of this country were copper-colored! When she spoke of driving near her own home the clergyman said:

"Er—may I ask if you drive the native animals?"

"'The native animals?'" the mystified lady echoed.

"Yes;—the elk, and moose, and buffalo, you know."

A notable "character" of the Wild West organization was Major Burke. He was so witty and genial that every one liked him at first sight. The Indians almost worshiped him and his authority over them was unquestioned. He had been made a member of one tribe by the "blood brotherhood" ceremony, but it had not needed this to make him regarded as "big medicine" by all the others. He had been associated with Buffalo Bill ever since "The Prairie Waif" days, and, though his nominal position with the Wild West was that of press-agent, he was an all-round and indispensable part of the management. His quick wits have served on many occasions to put an end to difficulties which less able men would have endured. For instance, on one occasion a number of women were standing on the front benches and obstructing the view of a hundred or more people behind them. Burke shouted,—though his voice was smooth and exquisitely modulated,—

"Will the beautiful young lady in front please sit down?" And twenty-eight women dropped as one.

Long before he went on the stage Colonel Cody had earned several desirable reputations in the West. One was as a stage-driver, in which capacity he was so much talked of that several Englishmen who went West insisted on riding in his coach. They made so much fuss about it, even in anticipation, that Bill resolved to give them a ride they would remember as long as they lived. His only special preparation was to fill his pockets with pebbles. The four mules started at a good pace, at which the passengers expressed delight. At the first down-grade, the driver pelted the mules furiously with the pebbles; their rough hides would have been insensible to the whip. Soon the pace became terrific, for the shower of pebbles continued; Cody looked back, saw the Englishmen huddled on the front seat, and shouted:

"Sit on the back seat!"

"It's no use, old chap," one of the frightened tourists replied. "We've just left there."

When Cody is not acting or riding or fighting Indians or ranching or asleep he is likely to be telling stories, and he has so many that it is hard for him to tell any story twice, unless by special request. One that has been frequently called for is of an Eastern man who was employed by Colonel Cody out West. The man had not been out long enough to know the illusive tricks of the clear atmosphere of the plains and hills. A picturesque mountain, that seemed only a mile away, interested him so greatly that he started early one morning to visit it and return by breakfast time. He didn't return for three days. A few days later the colonel saw him beside an irrigating ditch, and asked him what he was going to do, for the man was taking off his clothes.

"I'm goin' to swim across this river," was the reply.

"Swim? Why don't you jump it? It's only three feet wide."

"Ye-es; I know it looks that way, but I ain't goin' to be fooled again."

One evening, at the Hoffman House, he told this story to two or three friends with whom he was spending the evenings while he was General Sheridan's chief of scouts. There was "a little affair" in camp at which every one present got drunk but Cody; he had determined to keep sober, and succeeded. Toward morning he went to the cottage where he lived, rapped on the window, and made himself known, and his wife, who refused to open the door, said:

"Go away, whoever you are. Colonel Cody isn't home yet." At this point of the story Cody laughed and continued:

"Boys, I'd gone home sober, and my wife didn't know me! I went back to the camp, got as full as any one else, returned to my house, approached the door unsteadily, fumbled the latch, and my wife's voice greeted me, saying:

"'Is that you, Willie?'"

When this story ended, we started from the Hoffman House for the Lambs' Club, which was then in Twenty-sixth Street. With Cody and me were Steele Mackaye and Judge Gildersleeve, both of whom were tall, strong men. As we neared the club we met a crowd of very tough-looking men, and stood aside to let them pass, which they did, to my great relief. Then my companions got the laugh on me, for I remarked with earnest confidence:

"I'd like to see any four men get away with *us*!"

XIV
THE ART OF ENTERTAINING

Not as Easy as it Would Seem.—Scarcity of Good Stories for the Purpose.—Drawing-room Audiences are Fastidious.—Noted London Entertainers.—They are Guests of the People Who Engage Them.—London Methods and Fees.—Blunders of a Newly-wed Hostess from America.—Humor Displaces Sentiment in the Drawing-room.—My Own Material and Its Sources.

An entertainer always leaves a pleasant impression on other men; otherwise he is not an entertainer. Sometimes his gestures and manner are more effective than his words. Yet he is not necessarily an actor. He is a sort of half-brother of the man on the stage, for, like the actor, he must endeavor to please his entire audience. The humorous paper or book, if it is not to the reader's taste, may be dropped in an instant, but in a crowded hall or drawing-room one must listen, unless he is deaf.

So the entertainer must be very careful in selecting his material. Hundreds of jokes that are good in themselves and decent enough to tell to one's wife and children are called vulgar by some people who aren't noted for refinement in other ways. Other stories that are all right to try on your minister when you invite him to dinner, are shockingly irreverent to some folks who never go to church. Every man knows of honest hearty jokes that he wouldn't venture when ladies are present, but entertainers know of some stories told by good women that would make all the men in a drawing-room face toward the wall. Selecting stories for society is almost as dangerous as umpiring a baseball game.

John Parry was the original entertainer in England, a country so loyal to whoever amuses it that it honors its favorites, even after they have lost the power of pleasing. He wrote many sketches for use in drawing-rooms and became very popular and successful. The entertainers most in vogue in England, until recently, were Corney Grain, a six-footer, who died about three years ago and George Grossmith, whom many Americans remember and who was quite prominent in connection with D'Oyley Carte productions of the Gilbert and Sullivan operas. These gentlemen, both of fine appearance and manner, had their fill of engagements throughout the London season, going from one drawing-room to another and always hailed with delight. Their monologues never wearied, no matter how oft-repeated, for it is an amiable characteristic of the Englishman, that he can never get too much of a good thing. The American goes so far to the other extreme that he will stand something awfully bad if it is only new.

In England, the jester's arrangements are made with great ease and simplicity. There are no annoying business details. His terms of fifteen or twenty pounds an evening are already known, so money is not mentioned by him or his host and there is no attempt at "beating down," such as sometimes occurs in bargaining America. He goes to the house and the table as a guest and is treated as an equal by the hostess and her company, when he is making his adieus, which he does soon after completing his monologue, a sealed envelope is handed him, or the money reaches him at his hotel in the morning, and let me say right here for this custom, that in my own hundreds of English engagements I never lost a penny through bad pay.

Some of the more wealthy people do not limit themselves to the customary prices. For instance, Baron de Rothschild often pays sixty pounds for an entertainment not lasting more than ten minutes—a little matter of thirty dollars a minute, and by a strange coincidence, he never fails to get the entertainer he wants; some hosts do.

Most of my own London engagements are in May and June, up to July when the Goodwood races end the season. They are made some time in advance, the only preliminary on my part being a batch of letters I send off when my steamer reaches Queenstown. The fast mail reaches London before me, so by the time I reach my hotel, some replies are awaiting me. The receptions usually begin at ten in the evening. The hostess does not announce me formally, as if she owned me, body, soul and breeches, but asks graciously if Mr. Wilder will not kindly favor the company with some of his interesting experiences or reflections. Then I mount the piano, or a chair, if the affair is a dinner party, and the other guests listen politely, instead of all beginning to talk on their own account.

Entertainers almost never are subjected to snubs or other rudeness; when such unpleasantnesses occur they are promptly resented. An American woman who had "married into the nobility" invited me to come to her house at half past nine in the evening. I naturally assumed that this meant dinner. When I arrived, the flunkey took me into the parlor and left me there, saying Lady So-and-so and her guests were at dinner. I waited some moments, but as no one came to relieve me of my embarrassment, I rang the bell, requested the flunkey to take my card to his mistress and say I had been invited at that hour and had arrived. Word came back that "my lady" would be up in a few minutes. Then the ladies came into the drawing-room, leaving the gentlemen to their wine and cigars; those who knew me, the

Princess Mary of Teck was one of them, greeted me kindly, but my hostess and countrywoman did not seem to think me worthy of notice.

Then my American spirit rose to boiling point. I called my cab and was bowling down the street when a panting servant overtook me and gasped:

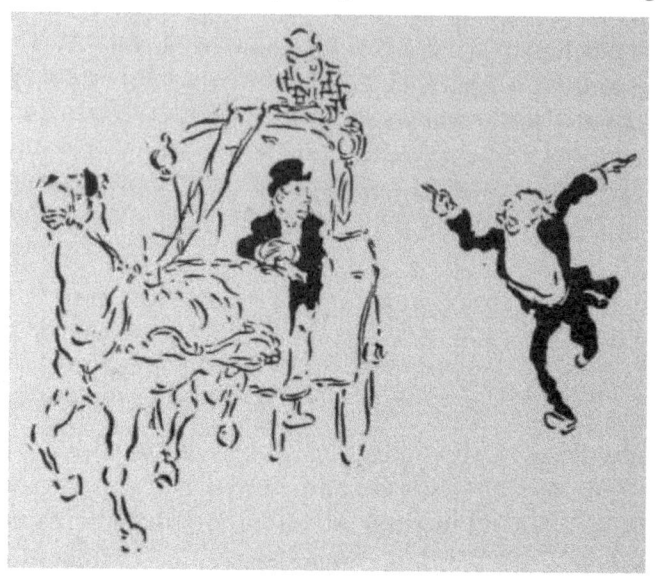

"My cab was bowling down the Street."

"Lady Blank would like to see you a moment, sir."

"Oh, would she?" I replied. When I returned I found the fair American in great distress. She wanted to know why I had deserted her at the critical moment, and when I told her bluntly that I was not in the habit of going to houses where I was not welcomed as a guest, she assured me her rudeness was unintentional, it was due to her ignorance of the custom, etc., etc., and she begged me not to leave her in the lurch. Of course, I pretended to be pacified, but the story got around London and did me much good, which is more than it did for her ladyship.

A peculiar thing about the English sense of humor is that although it is there and of full size, one must sometimes search hard to find it. Some types of American joking are utterly wasted on the Englishman.

The English greatly prefer burlesques on American characteristics to those on their own ways. I can't call this a peculiarity, although Americans specially like to see themselves and their own people "hit off," even if some one is hit hard. I am glad to say that although I am given to personalities, and exaggeration, I try never to cast ridicule on the people of whom I talk and I have never knowingly hurt any one's feelings by my character sketches.

In London the theatres are almost countless and are steadily increasing in number, and comedy, burlesque and farce are the rule—all because of the demand for fun. The English enjoy eating and sleeping more than any other people on earth, but English chops and sleep without some fun between, are as sounding brass and a tinkling cymbal, for dyspepsia will knock out the chops and insomnia will knock out sleep. But fun takes dyspepsia on one knee and insomnia on the other and bounces both into forgetfulness.

Since the days when Ward McAllister came into style, there has been a marked change in the work of the American jester. Time was, when here, as in England, any old thing would do for parlor entertainments, no matter how often it had been heard before. It did not even have to be funny, either; who can exaggerate the number of times he heard "Curfew Shall Not Ring To-night," in those good old times? Now, however, the entertainer must continually supply something new, or he will fall by the wayside. It must be something funny too; people used to crowd lecture rooms, and enjoy serious talks by great men—the greatest in the land, but whoever hears a lecture-course now? Fun—fun—fun, is the demand everywhere, so every entertainer is a joker.

In fact, to speak with my customary modesty, this demand for amusement places Mr. Depew and me on the same footing. Often I get letters from people who say they expect my friend the Senator, but, if he cannot come, will want me to fill the gap. Not long ago Mr. Depew cheated me out of a famous dinner at Delmonico's, so I grumbled a bit when I met him. He got off the big, hearty laugh, on which he has a life patent, with no possible infringement in sight, and replied,

"Why, Marsh, why didn't you tell me? If I'd known it, I wouldn't have gone."

"Enjoying serious talks by great men."

Ha, ha, pretty good, wasn't it?

Where do I get the material for my own sketches? From the originals every time. I pick it up in the streets, in the cars and restaurants, get it from the newsboys, from men of all sorts on the curb-stone, from almost everywhere, but never from books or newspapers, for the world is full of fun if one only has the ear to hear it.

When I get hold of a new thing that seems to be good, I always "try it on the dog"—that is, on my friends. I take it down to the Lambs' Club and work it off on some of the good fellows there. If I escape alive with it, I inveigle a couple of newsboys into a dark corner and have them sample it. If it "goes" with them, I am pretty sure it is good, so I add it to my repertoire; but if it fails there, I never disagree with my critics; it is damned—absolutely, no matter who may think it might be made to work.

Few Americans are busier than the successful entertainer. His hands are full of the work of brightening up the heavy parts of the social affairs that crowd the long winter afternoon and evenings, so with hurrying between New York, Boston and Chicago, with occasional moves to Philadelphia and Baltimore, he is kept "on the jump." Yet the public hears little of his work, for it is not advertised. Why, not long ago I went to a large party at a house only three blocks from my apartments, and I am sure thirty or forty of the guests had never heard my name before.

Such is fame.

XV
IN THE SUNSHINE WITH GREAT PREACHERS

I am Nicknamed "The Theological Comedian."—My Friend, Henry Ward Beecher.—Our Trip Through Scotland and Ireland.—His Quickness of Repartee.—He and Ingersoll Exchange Words.—Ingersoll's Own Sunshine.—De Witt Talmage on the Point of View.—He Could Even Laugh at Caricatures of His Own Face.—Dr. Parkhurst on Strict Denominationalism.

Nat Goodwin once nicknamed me "The Theological Comedian," because many of my entertainments were given in churches. On such occasions a minister would generally preface the proceedings with prayer—whether that I, or the people, might be strengthened for the ordeal I never was able to discover. But the ministers always laughed at every joke I cracked, so there is a very warm spot in my heart for them.

One of the first of the profession I ever met was Henry Ward Beecher. I became well acquainted with him and—of far more consequence, he was always friendly, fatherly and merry when I met him. I had the pleasure of traveling through Scotland and Ireland with him, and no man could have been better company. Yet he was not traveling merely for pleasure. Wherever he went and was known the people welcomed him effusively, insisted on hearing from him, so whenever he spoke in a church or Sunday-school he had a crowded house.

"Getting Properly Dismal for Sunday."

We spent one Sunday together in Glasgow, and the depression of that city on the holy day cannot be imagined. I have heard that some Scotchmen get full of bad whiskey on Saturday night for the sole purpose of being properly dismal on Sunday, but perhaps that is not true. But the street cars do not run; there is no sign of animation; the very houses look as dull as if they were untenanted; to a person accustomed to the cheer and bright faces of Americans on Sunday the town seemed enveloped in the gloom of death.

In the morning I awoke very early; I veritably believe that the appalling silence disturbed my slumbers. I felt so lonely and dismal that I instinctively went over to Mr. Beecher's room; better a drowsy American than a whole city full of wide-awake Scotchmen—on a Scotch Sunday. Mr. Beecher was also awake, though in bed, and in spite of the morning being quite chilly he lay with one toe uncovered. I said:

"Mr. Beecher, aren't you afraid of catching cold?"

"Oh, no," he replied, "I always sleep that way." I was greatly mystified at this, and asked him the reason. He laughed—and what a laugh he had! It was as big and solid and enduring as the Berkshire hills amid which he was born. Then he replied:

"Marshall, that toe is the key to the situation."

In Ireland we went about a good deal together in jaunting cars and extracted a lot of high-grade Hibernian wit from the drivers. Although Mr.

Beecher was one of the sensible souls who could discern the difference between poverty and misery, he had an American's innate soft spot in his heart for a man in rags, so he overpaid our drivers so enormously that Mrs. Beecher, who was with us, begged that she might be allowed to do the disbursing.

One day we were driven to our hotel in Belfast through a drizzling rain. When I paid the driver I said:

"Are you wet, Pat?" With a merry twinkle of his eye he replied:

"Sure, your honor, if I was as wet outside as I am inside, I'd be as dry as a bone."

Mr. Beecher's quickness at repartee, of which Americans knew well, was entirely equal to Irish demands upon it. One day in Ireland, after he had made an address to a Sunday-school, a bewitching young colleen came up to where we stood chatting and said:

"Mr. Beecher, you have won my heart."

"Well," replied the great man quickly, with a sunburst of a smile, "you can't get along without a heart, so suppose you take mine?"

Which reminds me of the day when he and Col. "Bob" Ingersoll were on the platform together at a public meeting and Beecher went over and shook hands heartily with the great agnostic, though he knew that the act would bring a storm of criticism from people with narrow-gauge souls. Then Ingersoll brought up one of his daughters and introduced her, saying:

"Mr. Beecher, here is a girl who never read the Bible." Bob delighted in shocking ministers, but he missed his fun that time, for Beecher quickly replied:

"If all heathen were so charming I am sure we should all become missionaries."

Ingersoll himself was as quick as the quickest at repartee. One day a malignant believer in an awful time for the wicked after death asked him:

"Are you trying to abolish hell?"

"If all Heathen were as Charming."

"Yes," said Ingersoll.

"Well, you can't do it."

"You'll be sorry if I don't," the Colonel replied.

Agnostic though he was, Ingersoll is frequently quoted by preachers, for in one respect he was very like the best of them; he never wearied of urging men to right living, not through fear of eternal punishment, but because goodness is its own excuse for being. No pastor was ever more severe than he in condemnation of everything mean and wicked in human life, so he was worthy of place among the great teachers of ethics. Personally he was as kind, sympathetic and helpful as some ministers are not; whatever he thought of systematic theology, he was practically a teacher of the brotherhood of man as defined by the founder of Christianity. In his lighter moments he was one of the merriest companions that any one could meet; no matter what he had to say, he would always illustrate it with a story. One day he was talking of people who have a knack of saying the right thing at the wrong time, and told the following, as a sample:

A well-to-do merchant out west lived in a town not remarkable for much but malaria and funerals. His wives had a way of dying, and whenever he lost one he went into another county and married again. A loquacious lady in the healthy county kindly assisted him in finding young women who were willing to marry him and take the chances. About six months after burying his fourth wife he appeared again in the healthy county, called on his friend and was greeted with:

"How's your wife, Mr. Thompson?"

"She's dead," he replied sadly.

"What? Dead again?" the woman cried.

Ingersoll was full of stories hinging on the place he believed did not exist. Here is one of them:

"His Wives had a Way of Dying."

A man who wanted to visit hell was advised to buy an excursion ticket. He did so, and when the train stopped at a place full of beautiful trees, warbling birds and bright sunshine he did not get off. The conductor said:

"I thought you wanted hell?"

"Is this hell?" the passenger asked; "I didn't think it looked like this." Then he walked about and met a man to whom he said:

"I am surprised to find hell such a beautiful place."

"Well," the man replied, "you must remember that there have been a great many clever people here for many years, so the place has greatly improved. You ought to have seen it when I came here."

"Indeed? And who are you?"

"I am Voltaire."

"I am very glad to meet you, Voltaire, and I wish you would do me a favor."

"With pleasure. What is it?"

"Get some one to buy my return ticket, please."

Colonel Ingersoll arrived late one evening at a Clover Club dinner in Philadelphia, to which he had been invited, and while looking for his seat he regarded the decorations so admiringly that Governor Bunn exclaimed:

"You've found heaven at last, Colonel, and a place waiting for you."

At a Lambs' Club dinner in New York, of which the late Steele MacKaye was chairman, Ingersoll was formally introduced and made a speech, in the course of which he made so unfortunate a remark about Deity that he sat down amid silence so profound as to be painful. MacKaye arose and with admirable tact brought the Club and the speaker en rapport by saying:

"Gentlemen, we all know that Colonel Ingersoll dare not believe in God, but those of us who know Colonel Ingersoll and do believe in God know that *God* believes in *him*."

The late T. DeWitt Talmage never lost a chance to emphasize a point with a good story. As I knew him to be a good man and a first-rate fellow, I used to be indignant at newspaper abuse of him, and particularly with some caricatures that were made of his expressive features. I took occasion to tell him of this, but he replied:

"Marshall, I'm as thick-skinned as a rhinoceros, and I never mind what is said about me. Some of the caricatures annoy me, but only because they pain people I love—my wife and family. You see, my boy, it doesn't pay to be too sensitive, for it breaks a man up, and that's the worst thing that can happen to him if he has any duties in the world. Besides, everything depends on the point of view. Once a German family emigrated to America and settled in Milwaukee. The oldest son, in his teens, concluded he would start out for himself. He 'fetched up' in New York, and without any money, so he wrote home, 'Dear father, I am sick and lonely and without a single cent. Send me some money quick. Your son John.' The old man couldn't read, so he took the letter to a friend—a great strapping butcher with a loud gruff voice and an arrogant manner of reading. When the letter was read to him the father was furious and declared he would not send his son a cent—not even to keep him from starving. But on his way home he kept thinking about the letter and wanting to hear it again, so he took it to another friend—a consumptive undertaker who had a gentle voice with an appealing inflection in it. When this man read the letter the father burst into tears and exclaimed, 'My poor boy! I shall send him all the money he wants.' You see, the same thing viewed from a different point takes on a different color."

After the Rev. Dr. Parkhurst visited some notorious New York "dives" and preached his famous sermon on New York politics he was the sensation of the day and also one of the best abused men in the land. He was besieged by reporters until he had scarcely time to say his prayers and came to hate the sight of a newspaper man. About that time I was making a trip to Rochester and saw Dr. Parkhurst enter the car I was in. I said to some friends:

"That is Dr. Parkhurst. Now watch me; I'm going to have some fun with him."

His chair was at the other end of the car and he was having a good time with newspapers and magazines and far away, as he supposed, from reporters. I passed and repassed him two or three times; then, assuming as well as I could the manner of a newspaper man I stopped and said:

"Dr. Parkhurst, I believe?"

He looked up with a savage frown, and I saw that he took me for one of the tormenting fraternity. I continued in an insinuating, tooth-drawing manner until he became so chilling that I could hear the thermometer falling with heavy thuds. When I felt that I had made him as uncomfortable as I could I said,

"Pardon me, Doctor, but evidently you don't remember me." Then I handed him my card. His manner changed like a cloudy day when the sun breaks through, and he said cordially:

"I am glad to see you, Mr. Wilder. I mistook you for a reporter."

"I thought, you would," I replied, "for that's what I was trying to make you believe."

We laughed together and for the remainder of the trip we were close companions. He is a delightful talker, full of anecdotes and reminiscences. I never met a keener lover of good stories than he, and, beside being an appreciative listener, he is so good a raconteur himself that a listener is willing that he should do all the story telling. He has no patience with narrow, hide-bound denominationalists; he defined them by telling me a story of a minister who preached a sermon so touching that all his hearers were melted to tears—all but one man. When asked how he had succeeded in keeping his eyes dry the man replied:

"Well, you see, this isn't my church."

XVI
THE PRINCE OF WALES
(*Now King Edward VII*)

The Most Popular Sovereign in Europe.—How He Saved Me From a Master of Ceremonies.—Promotion by Name.—He and His Friends Delight two American Girls.—His Sons and Daughters.—An Attentive and Loving Father.—Untiring at His Many Duties Before He Ascended the Throne.—Unobtrusive Politically, yet Influential.

If all kings were as competent as the genial and tactful gentleman who recently ascended the British throne, it would be a thankless job to start a new republic anywhere. Personally, I have strong grounds for this opinion, for I had the pleasure of meeting His Majesty many times while he was Prince of Wales, and these meetings were due entirely to his kindness of nature and generally were of his own initiative.

I don't imagine he knew it, but the Prince of Wales once lifted me out of as uncomfortable a fix as I ever got into in London. The Ancient and Honorable Artillery, Boston's swell military organization, visited England in 1896, as guests of the Ancients and Honorables of London, who entertained them handsomely and had them presented to Her Majesty the queen. The Boston company in turn, gave a great dinner to their hosts. Some Americans then in the city were invited, and I had the good fortune to be of the number, through the kindness of Mr. B. F. Keith, who was one of the Boston Ancient and Honorables.

The spectacle was brilliant in the extreme, nine out of every ten men present being in full dress uniform. The entire assemblage was gathered informally in two long, glittering rows, awaiting the Prince of Wales, who was always the soul of punctuality. I had many acquaintances in the two uniformed bodies, as well as among the non-military guests, and was moving about from one to another. I was in conventional evening dress, and had a tiny American flag pinned to the lapel of my coat.

The Master of Ceremonies, whose manner was more consequential than that of any distinguished person in the room, seemed annoyed that any civilians were present, and he did his utmost to separate them from the soldiers. I had the misfortune to become his *bête noire*; whenever he found me among the military men he gently but persistently pressed me away, but no sooner did he eject me in one direction than I reappeared from another and between two pairs of gaily-appareled soldiers' legs, so I made the poor fellow nervous and fussy to the verge of distraction.

"I had the misfortune to become his *bête noire*."

Exactly at eight o'clock the Prince of Wales was announced and every one came to attention. He entered with the genial smile which was an inseparable part of him and shook hands with the American minister and other dignitaries. Soon he spied me, came across the room, greeted me very kindly, and said:

"How are you, little chap?"

"Very well, thank you, sir," I replied.

"I am to hear you to-morrow night at the Duke of Devonshire's, I understand," he continued. "Won't you give us that mother-in-law pantomime of yours?"

"Certainly, sir," I answered; as the Prince left me and ascended the stairs I saw that the Master of Ceremonies, who had witnessed the meeting, was visibly disturbed. Soon he literally hovered about me and displayed a fixed and conciliatory smile. The guests began to follow the Prince, and as they passed up the stairs many of them greeted me. Senator Depew remarked:

"Hello, Marshall, how are you?"

That dear old gentleman and English idol, John L. Toole, passed, blinked merrily at me and said:

"Glad to see you again, Marshall. How are you?"

Presently the Master of Ceremonies turned nervously to an English officer and asked, with an aggrieved tone in his voice:

"Who is this little chap, anyway? Everybody seems to know him."

The officer did not chance to know me, but an English Sergeant who was of the attendant guard and was willing to impart information said:

"He belongs to the American Army. He's a marshal." The great functionary immediately regarded me with profound respect, not unmixed with wonder at the modesty of great American soldiers, for an officer of my supposedly exalted rank was entitled to follow close behind His Royal Highness.

"They regarded me with profound respect."

At the Duke of Devonshire's on the following evening I was assisted by two young Americans—twin sisters, the Misses Jessie and Bessie Abbot. Miss Bessie had a wonderful voice, and has since achieved a great success in Paris in the title part of the opera "Juliet." Both girls were clever and charming and we three maintained a friendship which was delightful to me and which they, too, seemed to enjoy. At that time they were living in London with their mother, and taking part in private entertainments, but the evening at the Duke of Devonshire's was their first appearance before the Prince of Wales or any of the Royal family. They charmed the audience and were loaded with compliments, some of which were expressed by the Princess of Wales in person.

While the Princess was conversing with the sisters she mentioned the Prince, upon which Miss Jessie said:

"I have not yet met the Prince, but I wish to very much."

"Oh, have you not?" the Princess exclaimed, as she smilingly regarded the pretty girl who was unconscious that she had committed a breach of etiquette. "Then I shall arrange it." Immediately she walked the entire length of the long picture gallery in which the entertainment had been given, found the Prince, came back on his arm, and Miss Jessie's request was granted. The Prince, noting the resemblance of the sisters to each other, asked if they were really twins.

"Oh, yes," Miss Jessie replied, and then turning to me she continued, "Aren't we, Marshall? Her ingenuous manner compelled the Prince to laugh, after which he said to me:

"You seemed to be posted, little chap."

Among royal children whom I have had the honor to entertain, none are more widely known, through their portraits and also by common report, than the sons and daughters of the present King and Queen of England. The first time I ever appeared before them was at an exhibition given for the benefit of the Gordon home for boys. It was a social affair of great prominence, the audience being composed principally of the royal family and the nobility. The Prince and Princess of Wales were accompanied by their children—Prince Albert Victor, who has since died but was then heir-apparent, Prince George, who is now Prince of Wales, and the Princesses Louise, Victoria and Maude. Other members of the royal family in the audience were the Duke of Connaught (brother to the Prince), the Duke and Duchess of Teck and the Princess Louise of Teck.

I suppose I ought to do the conventional thing by likening King Edward's daughters to Washington Irving's "Three Beautiful Princesses," but my first impression of them has remained clear that I frequently revert to the day I received it—three wholesome, pretty, dainty English little girls of demure manner, with exquisite complexions, and whose blonde hair was very long and their simple white frocks rather short. They had many points of resemblance to one another, but their brothers were quite dissimilar in one respect, Victor being slight and delicate while George was sturdy and robust. All seemed to enjoy the entertainment, but did not forget and lose control of themselves, as well-bred American children sometimes do in public. Princess Louise of Teck, who is considered the handsomest of the princesses, was at that time a very beautiful and attractive child.

I afterward met them all at the Duke of Devonshire's and found that in conversation with their elders their manner was marked by the simplicity, thoughtfulness and kindness inseparable from good breeding. They frequently rode or drove in the park, accompanied by a lady-in-waiting or a gentleman of the Queen's household. The universal respect manifested for them did not turn their heads in the least; in acknowledgment of the bared heads about them they did not bow haughtily, but graciously and kindly, as if grateful for the attention bestowed upon them. It seemed impossible, to any one who had observed the condescending and even arrogant manner in public of so many English children whose dress and equipage indicated parental wealth and station, that the Prince of Wales's children could be what they really were—scions of the most firmly-rooted royal stock in all Europe and that from among them would in time come an occupant of the only throne whose influence is felt entirely around the world.

But the key to the mystery was not far to find; one had but to go back to the parents of these model children—to the Prince of Wales and his consort, the daughter of a king whose tact and sense are universally recognized and admired and who to this day, although past his eighty-sixth birthday, is a model for rulers everywhere. The Prince of Wales was, as under his new title of King Edward he still is, as affectionate and attentive a father as can be found in the world. Despite common report, founded on his affable and leisurely manner in public, he has for many years been a close student of affairs and a very busy man, yet there never was a time when his children had not free access to him, nor when he was not his children's industrious teacher and mentor. For years he has been known as the most tactful man in England, and without a superior in this respect in the world. Speaking literally, royalty is his life business; it is also to be the life-business of his children, so he has made it a matter of sense as well as of duty that his sons and daughters should be prepared to so comport themselves as to make their royalty secure and themselves safe. History has taught him that neither great armies nor well-filled coffers can maintain a family on the throne, and that the only security of a ruler is found in the respect and affection of the people. While his mother was on the throne he probably heard thousands of times—indirectly, of course, the common prediction of "advanced" politicians that he never would succeed her. Probably this prediction never caused him to lose a single hour of sleep, for he never allowed himself to neglect one of the thousands of duties that devolved upon him as his mother's personal representative. Never obtrusive politically, he nevertheless became a positive influence in national politics; he appeared at all public functions that asked royal sanction, always said and did the right thing, made himself approachable, always was affable though never lacking in dignity, and gave to every man, great or simple, the full measure of attention and respect that was due him, seasoning the same so thoroughly with courtesy as to make a lifelong admirer of the receiver. He imparted his manner to his sons and daughters and his consort added to his influence by motherly training similar to his own. No breath of scandal has ever touched one of these children; in this respect the family is almost unique, for black sheep are prominent in almost all royal families of

Europe, and one such character is enough to inflict a lasting smirch on the entire house.

The Prince of Wales whom I met is now King of England and his children are men and women. His official presence is overshadowing his unofficial past, almost to the extent of forgetfulness. But no thoughtful observer will forget that King Edward and his children as they now appear date back to many years of His Majesty's life when he was Prince of Wales and in apparent likelihood of being outlived by his mother.

XVII
SIR HENRY IRVING

A Model of Courtesy and Kindness.—An Early Friend Surprised by the Nature of His Recognition.—His Tender Regard for Members of His Company.—Hamlet's Ghost Forgets His Cue.—Quick to Aid the Needy.—Two Lucky Boys.—Irving as a Joker.—The Story He Never Told Me.—Generous Offer to a Brother Actor-manager.—Why He is Not Rich.

The American people at large know Henry Irving as a great actor, scores of Americans and hundreds of Englishmen of his own and related professions know him as one of the most friendly and great-hearted men alive. Many volumes could be written about his thoughtful kindnesses, and at least one of them could be filled with mention of his goodness to me, for, in my many visits to England, he never failed to "look me up" and show me every kindness in his power—and his power is great. If I were to go into details regarding myself, I should offend him, for, like any other genuine man, he does not like his left hand know what his right hand does, but it shouldn't hurt for me to tell some open secrets about his kindness to others.

Lionel Brough often talks of the time when he and Irving, both of them young men, were members of a company in Manchester. In those days Irving was a dreamer of dreams and had a fondness for being his own only company, so his associates made him the butt of many jokes that did not seem to disturb his self-absorption. He had no intimates in the company, although he was of lovable nature. Near the theatre was an upholstery shop, the owner of which became acquainted with Irving, understood him and loved him, as did the family; they called the young actor "Our Henry," always had room and a hearty welcome for him, and in many ways served as balm to his sensitive nature.

When Irving went to London he did not forget his Manchester friends—not even after he became a successful and very busy manager. He sent them frequent evidences of his regard, though he had no time to make visits. On coming into possession of the Lyceum Theatre he determined to reupholster every part of it. A large London firm desired the contract and made estimates but Mr. Irving sent to Manchester for his old friend, and, as the Irving company was leaving England for a long American tour, gave the upholsterer *carte blanche*.

On Irving's return from America be inspected his theatre, was delighted with the renovation, and asked the upholsterer for the bill. After looking it over he sent for the London firm that had offered plans and estimates, and asked them what they would have charged to do what had been done. They named a sum five times as large as the Manchester man had charged; Irving discovered later that his old friend had charged only for materials, the work being "thrown in" for old affection's sake. But Irving disregarded the bill entirely and drew a check for twice the amount of the London firm's estimate.

But it does not require memories of past kindnesses to open Mr. Irving's purse, for he is almost as susceptible to the influence of old association. He has always maintained a far larger company than his productions demanded, and retained old members long after their services would have been dispensed with by a manager at all careful of his pennies. Many Americans have pleasant remembrances of old "Daddy" Howe, who died in Cincinnati some years ago while a member of the Irving company on tour. At a memorable dinner given Mr. Irving by his professional admirers in America, Mr. Howe arose and told of his offering to retire when the company was preparing to come to this country, and how his suggestion was received. Although he was eighty years old at the time, he had been a member of but three companies, one of which was Mr. Irving's. He knew that the expenses of the American tour would be enormous, and that the small parts for which he was usually cast would be well played here for far less than his own salary, so his conscience compelled him to write Mr. Irving saying that he comprehended the situation and would either retire or accept less pay. As he received no reply, he repeated his suggestion in person to Mr. Irving.

"Dear me!—Ah! yes!—Well, I'll let you know presently," was the evasive answer from which Howe assumed that he would be retired, so it was with trembling hands that he opened a note from the manager the next day. He read:

"Of course I expect you to go to America, and I hope the increase of your salary will indicate my appreciation and good wishes."

As Howe told this story his eyes filled and overflowed, but Irving, when all eyes were turned toward him, looked as if he did not see that there was anything in the incident to justify the old actor's emotion or the applause of every one around the tables.

I am indebted to my friend, Mr. J. E. Dodson, who came over with Mrs. Kendall's company, for these stories illustrating Mr. Irving's manner on the stage in circumstances which would make almost any manager star drop into rage and profanity. Here is one of them:

"Old Tom Meade, beloved by all English players, and the best stock ghost any company ever had, was much given to reading in the dressing-room between his cues. "Hamlet" was on one night, and after his first appearance as the murdered king, Meade went to his room for the long "wait" before the closet scene. With his heels on the table, a black clay pipe in his mouth and silver spectacles astride his nose he was soon in the profoundest depths of a philosophical work. The call boy gave him notice of his cue.

"Uh-yes," was the reply, but Meade went on reading. Several minutes later there was feverish excitement in the wings and messengers from the stage manager poured into Meade's room; the lights had been lowered, the stage was enveloped in blue haze, but there was no ghost! Dropping his book, Meade hurried to the stage, but in his excitement he entered on the wrong side, and almost behind Hamlet. It was too late to go around to the other side, so Meade whispered huskily to Mr. Irving:

"Here, sir, here—just behind you!"

About this time the man who managed the calcium light succeeded in locating the dilatory ghost and in throwing the blue haze upon him, as Hamlet exclaimed:

"See where he goes e'en now, out at the portal!"

Poor Meade was in agony until he was able to speak to Mr. Irving.

"Gov'n'r," he faltered, "reading in my dressing-room—heard call, but forgot. Rushed to wrong side of stage, sir. Never happened before—never will again, sir. And after all, it didn't go so bad, sir." For a moment Mr. Irving looked him through and through, after which he said icily:

"Yes, Tom—but I like it better the other way."

One day Mr. Irving chanced to meet McIntyre, with whom he had played in the provinces in his own struggling days. The two men had not met in years, and Irving's eyes—marvelous eyes they are, beamed with delight, as they always do when they see an old companion.

"Well, well, McIntyre!" he exclaimed. "What are you doing here?"—and he led the way into Haxell's, where they might have a quiet chat over cigars and brandy and soda.

"Nothing," was the comprehensive reply.

"Have you settled on anything?"

McIntyre admitted that he was expecting to play in something at the Holborn. Before they parted Irving said: "You must come down and have seats in the house, so you can tell me what you think of us." Next day he sent to the Holborn a most cordial letter containing tickets for the two best seats in the lyceum and an urgent request for another chat. Merely as an afterthought was this postscript:

"Forgive me for handing you a ten-pound note as a loan at your convenience. You may need to get something new for the play." McIntyre's feelings may be imagined when I repeat his confession that at that moment he did not know where his next meal was coming from.

Mr. Irving is very fond of children and—as does not always follow in other men's fondness of the same nature, he is very attentive to them. When he produced "Olivia," the juvenile part was played by a nine year old boy who kept himself very clean and tidy, but his street clothes were so old that extreme poverty was evident. One night Mr. Irving asked:

"Where do you live, my lad?"

"Beyond Hammersmith, sir"—a London section some miles from the theatre.

"And how do you get home?"

"I walk, sir," the boy replied, surprised by the inquiry.

"Yes, yes. But after this you must ride"—and Mr. Irving ordered that the boy should be supplied with bus fares thereafter. Later Mr. Irving noticed that the boy had a troubled look on his face. Asked if he didn't enjoy riding, he confessed that he had been walking to save his 'bus fares, for his mother was ill and his father out of work. An order was given that the boy's salary should be raised; throughout the summer, though the company was not playing, the child continued to receive his salary, at Irving's personal order.

Still more significant of his cherishing regard for children is a story of how he squandered time—more carefully guarded on the stage than anything else,—to make a boy happy. It occurred in a one-act piece—"Cramond Brig," in which there is a supper-scene in a cottage, a steaming sheep's head and an oat-cake are brought in and the cottar's little son is supposed to do boyish justice to the feast. The little chap who played the part did not look as if he had eaten more than his allowance, which was not to be wondered at; stage feasts are not prepared by chefs, and the sheep's head was indifferently cooked, the only stage demand being that it should send up a cloud of steam and look piping hot. One night, when the meat chanced to be well cooked, Mr. Irving noted that the boy entered into the spirit of the scene with extreme realism, so with a smile at the youngster's energy he asked:

"Like it, me boy? Ah, yes; I thought so. Boys are always hungry."

No sooner was that hungry boy out of hearing than Mr. Irving ordered that the sheep's head and oat-cake should in future be properly seasoned and carefully cooked; still more, he informed the players that the supper-scene was not to be hurried, but was to be governed by the boy's appetite. And how that boy did enjoy the change!—though Mr. Irving seemed to get as much pleasure out of the feast as he.

"Old John," Irving's personal servant and dressing-room valet, used to go on a spree about once a year. With the fatality peculiar to such men, his weakness took possession of him on a night of "The Lyon's Mail"—a play in which the leading character must make so rapid a change that quick and sober hands must assist him. Just as the change was impending poor John stole into the theatre and stood in the wings with comb, brush and other necessary articles hugged to his breast, though he was plainly incompetent to use them. He cut a ludicrous figure, though the time was not one for fun—not for the star. Mr. Irving grasped the situation; almost any other actor in similar circumstances would have grasped the valet also and shaken the life out of him. Irving merely said mildly—very mildly:

"John, you're tired. Go home."

Almost any man possessing a sense of humor has one and only one way of manifesting it, but in humor as on the stage Mr. Irving is protean. In the course of a long chat which he and Richard Mansfield had one night at the Garrick Club, Mansfield spoke of his noted Jekyll-and-Hyde part, which was very long yet called for but two notes of his voice—a severe physical strain, and he said:

"John, you're tired."

"You know, Mr. Irving, it is longer than your great speech in Macbeth. I have been advised by our New York physicians not to do it."

Irving looked thoughtful for a moment or two, which is a long period of silence for an eloquent man. Then he asked:

"My boy, why *do* you do it?"

Members of the Dramatists' Club (New York) still recall with delight a story he once told them and which promised a brilliant climax that they could distinctly foresee. The end was quite as effective as they had imagined, yet it was entirely different and consisted of but two words.

Irving can turn even his peculiarities to account in story-telling. Like any other man of affairs he had sudden and long periods of absent-mindedness—which means that his mind is for the time being not only not absent but on the contrary is entirely present and working at the rate of an hour a minute. One day while we were driving together he turned to me and said:

"Marshall, I have a story you can add to your repertoire—a very quaint one." Then he went into deep thought and we had gone fully a block before he spoke again; then he said:

"And you know——"

Then we went another block, then farther, but suddenly he asked:

"Now wasn't that droll?" It certainly was, no matter what it was, if he said so, but he still owes me the story, for he had told it only to himself.

Such details of Irving's thoughtfulness—almost fatherly solicitude, for other members of his profession, as have become generally known are but a small fraction of what might be told had not the beneficiaries been begged to hold their tongues. But here is one that was made public by my friend, E. S. Willard, an English actor already referred to and very popular in America. To realize its significance, one must imagine himself an American manager with an appreciative eye for Lyceum successes. At a dinner given at Delmonico's by Willard to Irving, Mr. Willard said:

"When he heard of my first venture into the United States, Mr. Irving, without telling me of it, wrote a lot of friends over here that I was not a bad sort of chap, and they might look after me a bit. He gathered around me the night before I left London, a lot of his friends whom he knew I would like to meet. When I was about to leave the room he took me aside and said:

"'If you find when you get to the other side that your plays don't carry, or that the American people don't take to them, just cable me one word. Here is my new play at the Lyceum, a beautiful success, and you shall have it—words, music and all, as soon as the steamer can get it to you.'"

"My boy, why *do* you do it?"

It is not generally known that before being knighted Sir Henry Irving had twice refused a title, and accepted only after he had been convinced, by men prominent in other professions, that his "elevation," as the English call it, would redound to the benefit of the profession at large. Personally the rank could have placed him no higher socially than he already was, for ever since he became known he has been surrounded by an aristocracy of brains. He will not and cannot be patronized, and, through the lasting respect which he has earned, he has done wonders for the dignity of the actors' calling. His title has not changed his manner in any way. His great dinners on the stage of the Lyceum and his lunches at the Beefsteak Club are matters of history. His social engagements are as numerous as ever; often he does not retire until three or four o'clock in the morning, generally to arise in time to conduct a rehearsal at ten, so his duties require an executive genius equal in degree to his artistic endowment.

It is strange to many people that a man of Mr. Irving's business ability and personal popularity should be in comparatively poor circumstances instead of having acquired a fortune. He lives plainly, in hired rooms, not indulging in the luxury of a house of his own, with horses, carriages, etc. He spends money freely for books, and professionally for anything that may enhance the effect of his art and that of his theatre. But the few incidents cited above, are illustrations of the manner in which thousands of pounds have leaked from his pockets and show that it is bigness of heart that keeps Henry Irving from being a rich man.

XVIII
LONDON THEATRES AND THEATRE-GOERS

Why English and American Plays do Best at Home.—The Intelligent Londoner Takes the Theatre Seriously.—Play-going as a Duty.—The High-class English Theatre a Costly Luxury.—American Comedies Too Rapid of Action to Please the English.—Bronson Howard's "Henrietta" Not Understood in London.—The Late Clement Scott's Influence and Personality.

I believe I can explain why most English plays have failed to please American audiences, and that I have discovered the reason of the appalling apathy with which Londoners usually receive an American play.

When I say "Londoners" I refer to the better class. The common people flock to the comedies, farces and burlesques, of which London is full; they laugh at whatever is placed before them and demand a lot more of the same kind. But the educated, well-bred Englishman makes a serious matter of theatre-going. He goes to the play with the same face that he displays in "the city," as the business section of London is called. He changes his clothes, for it is bad form not to be in evening dress when one goes to a London theatre of the better class. But he does not change his face. Play-going is as much a duty with him, as business is, and I am inclined to believe it is quite as much of a bore. However that may be, it is a matter of his serious daily routine. He goes to the theatre to think; goes as solemnly as an American on his way to church.

Indeed, the talk one overhears in the lobby and stalls of a high class English theatre recall some church experiences to an American. The play is analyzed; so are its parts, as if the whole thing were a matter of conscience or morals, as occasionally it is. A "problem" play which would drive Americans out of a theatre, unless in Boston, where they would doze through the performance, trusting to the morning papers for points enough to talk about, will make its way to the profoundest depths of the English heart and head.

It must not be inferred that English gentlemen and ladies do not enjoy good comedies. They are grateful for anything that is humorous and witty, but they regard such performances as mere relishes or dessert; the *pièce de résistance* must be solid.

The best London audiences are drawn from the fashionable set—the "smart set," all members of which attend the theatre whenever their evenings are unoccupied by social duties. There are no matinées—by name; the English say "morning performance," which means the same thing; and of course "morning" means afternoon, for the fashionable set turn night into day so successfully, that the old fashioned morning is gone before they get out of bed.

"He reads what the papers say about it."

Only a man of good income can afford steady theatre-going on the English plan. His seat costs him about $2.75, and his program twenty-five cents more; to these expenses must be added cab fares both ways, for your Londoner won't walk more than a block after dark, if he can help it. After he has seen and heard the performance he talks a lot about it, and thinks it over, and next day reads what the papers say about it, and these say as much and say it as seriously as if the playhouses were of as much importance as the House of Parliament. Only recently have American literary weeklies taken up the theatres, but the Englishman has seen solemn critiques of plays in the *Athenæum* and *Academy* ever since he began to read those papers.

The well-to-do American wants change, relaxation and fun when he goes to the theatre. He is fully as intellectual as his English cousin and has quite as keen comprehension of the best dramatic work; this is proved by his enthusiastic support of all productions of Shakespeare. But a coldly correct drama with a sad end does not appeal to him, no matter how good the acting.

American plays are usually too compact and too rapid of action to succeed on the English stage. Bronson Howard's brilliant "Henrietta" was highly praised by the London press and Londoners loyally try to like whatever their newspaper tells them to. Yet "The Henrietta" did not quite suit. The audience simply could not understand the character of "Bertie" the millionaire's indolent, cheery, stupid son who pretended to be a devil of a fellow at his club, but really had no head for liquor and tobacco nor any heart for the society of chorus girls. London society has many young men with some one of Bertie's peculiarities, but the combination—why, as one Londoner said: "No chap can be so many things, don't you know."

Even Mr. J. L. Shine, the accomplished actor who played the part, did not seem to understand it. Another mistake was with "The little English Lord," as he was called in the play—a lordling whom a rich American girl had married. Here he was a fussy little fellow, an undersized dude—a caricature, in fact, and made no end of fun, but on the London stage he was the real thing, and taken seriously. The management seemed to be afraid to travesty so sacred a personage as a noble lord. I imagine this was a mistake, for at least a portion of the British people had been so far emancipated as to appreciate fun poked at the "hupper classes."

I have mentioned London's respect for dramatic criticism. Let us admit for a moment that London is the centre of the universe—the great wheel that sets all the rest in motion, and that what is successful there ought to succeed everywhere else—even if it doesn't. Then, in logical sequence, let us understand that the greatest critic of the metropolis can make or break any "attraction," and that this commanding position was held by the late Clement Scott,—poet, *littérateur* and playwright, for more than a quarter of a century and have we not practically admitted that Mr. Scott was theatrical dictator of the universe?

Even logic is sometimes at fault. I remember being taught at school that dry bread was better than heaven, because dry bread is better than nothing and nothing is better than heaven—see? This is not cited to imply that what I have said of Clement Scott is wrong, but to convince the skeptical that all men cannot be expected to reason alike.

There was no doubt of the greatness of the London *Daily Telegraph's* critic, for nothing was easier of comprehension. He was a master of word-painting; the grace and truthfulness of his word-pictures were evident to the most careless reader. There was nothing vulgar or flippant in anything he wrote, and irrelevant witticisms, such as many would-be critics indulge in, were entirely lacking in his work. Slow to condemn, when he corrected a player the work was done with gracious gentleness, although his satire, when needed, was biting and deep. In the righting of wrongs he proved himself utterly fearless, and regardless of consequences to himself. By this course he made many friends and more enemies. Indeed, one of his peculiarities was his readiness to make an enemy, if by so doing he could win a friend.

Mr. Scott was truly a friend to the friendless, a helper of the helpless and a clever adviser to all. Both he and his wife were very active in charitable work, but his greatest energies seemed to have been exerted in securing employment for needy actors and aiding aspiring ones by word and deed, for he did so much for both classes that his friends wondered how he found time for anything else. His kindness knew no bounds of nation or tongue, and the antagonism supposed to exist between Englishmen and Americans found no echo in his big heart.

In appearance Mr. Scott resembled a rugged oak-tree that has grown so vigorously in all directions that any part seems fully as strong as any other. He was rather tall, with broad shoulders that drooped slightly, and was quite fleshy although not obese. His ears were set far back on his head and his face, though intellectual, was largely modeled—high forehead, heavy eyebrows, kind and thoughtful gray eyes, a large nose and mouth and in his later years a white moustache. His hands, though large, were so shapely as to command attention.

In manner he was emphatic but never dogmatic, as some members of his profession are. His prominence was greater than can be imagined in the United States, where the people seldom know the names of the dramatic critics whose work they most admire, yet he was as modest and unaffected as any of his admirers. There was nothing of the *ergo ego* about him, nor anything pretentious. Yet there lurked behind his mild, quiet manner an enthusiasm for work and a scholarly application to work, that were absolutely remarkable. At the theatre he was the last man whom a stranger would suspect of being a critic, for the bored look and the feigned weariness that some of the dramatic reviewers affect were entirely lacking in him. He did not even make notes on his programme. Men like Scott do not have to affect wisdom or the resigned look that is supposed to result from it. I know a young whipper-snapper with a nice, fast-black bored look that cost years of effort to cultivate. He is said to wrap it in a silk handkerchief and keep it in a bureau drawer when not in use, but he never forgets to dust it and have it properly adjusted when he calls on a lady or attends the theatre.

Clement Scott was not that kind of man. He had some little peculiarities, like all men of genius but they were neither affected nor obtrusive. The most noticeable of these was a habit of saying "yes, yes," and "what?" continually. Some of his gestures were a bit odd and he had an amusing way of belittling his own work. He said to me one day,

"I make no money from my books. It is all I can do to give them away."

"A nice fast-black bored look that cost years of effort to cultivate."

He had the coziest possible little home at 15 Woburn Square, London, and a wife who would reflect honor on any mansion in the land. Her portrait hangs before me while I write—the face of an intelligent, refined, charming English lady, and on its margin is written "Yours in all faith, Margaret Clement Scott." That describes her perfectly—"in all faith" she was the best possible helper to her husband, aiding him in his correspondence, taking proper care of his memoranda, writing at his dictation and assisting him in many other ways.

In Mr. Scott's study were many hundred valuable books, some of which are very rare, and a great collection of curios. One of the walls was hung with old prints of noted theatrical people of earlier generations; another with fine china. The room was richly furnished and had an air of oriental luxury which, combined with picturesque disorder, was more than charming—it was bewilderingly bewitching. In one corner was an interesting souvenir in a frame; his first letter of credential as dramatic critic, and was given by the *Sunday Times*, with which he was first connected; he went to the *Telegraph* in 1872.

Mr. Scott was playwright as well as critic and had several plays successfully produced—"Tears, Idle Tears," an adaptation from Marcel; "Peril," taken from Sardou's "Nos Intimes," "Diplomacy," written in collaboration with B. C. Stephenson; "Sister Mary," of which Wilson Barrett was part author; "Jack in the Box" (with George R. Sims); "The Cape Mail," "Serge Panine," adapted from Georges Ohnet for Mrs. Langtry, "The Swordsman's Daughter," in which Brandon Thomas had a hand and "Denise," in collaboration with Sir Augustus Harris. Among his published books are "Round About the Islands"; "Poppyland"; "Pictures of the World"; "Among the Apple Orchards"; "Over the Hills and Far away"; "The Land of Flowers"; "Thirty Years at the Play"; "Dramatic Table Talk"; "The Wheel of Life"; "Lays of a Londoner"; "Lays and Lyrics"; "Theatrical Addresses" and his famous "Patriot Songs."

XIX
TACT

An Important Factor of Success.—Better than Diplomacy.—Some Noted Possessors of Tact.—James G. Blaine.—King Edward VII.—Queen Alexandra.—Henry Ward Beecher.—Mme. Patti.—Mrs. Ronalds.—Mrs. Cleveland—Mrs. Langtry.—Colonel Ingersoll.—Mrs. Kendall.—General Sherman.—Chauncey M. Depew.—Mrs. James Brown Potter.—Mme. Nordica.

I have had the good fortune to meet a great many distinguished people, and the misfortune of hearing many of these talked of afterward as if human greatness was merely a machine, which had some peculiar secret of motion. I don't like to listen to analyses of my friends and acquaintances; it is too much like vivisection; it is unkind to the subject and hardens whoever conducts the operation.

Besides, I have a theory of my own as to greatness. It is that tact is generally the secret. Almost all famous men and women admit that certain other people are superior to them at their own special work. They will attribute some of their success to luck and some to accident, but the close observer can usually see that tact has had far more influence than either, for success depends largely on getting along well with other people, and nothing but tact can assure this.

Diplomacy alone cannot take the place of tact, for it comes only from the head; tact is from the heart. The prominent people to whom I refer did not lack great qualities of head; they would have failed without them, but these alone would have been insufficient without the softer sense—"The inmost one," as Hawthorne named it; the quality to which Oliver Wendell Holmes referred when he said—"I am getting in by the side door." Diplomacy, as distinguished from tact, is something with a string to it: or playing for a place; tact is a subtle, timely touch from the heart.

A few years ago I returned from Europe on the steamer with Mr. James G. Blaine. Every one on board wanted to talk with him and learn of things which taste and prudence forbade his mentioning. Yet Mr. Blaine was so tactful throughout this ordeal, that no one suffered a rebuff and every one became his friend. He went further by discovering the good but shrinking people who in a great ship became isolated, and bringing them into the general company and conversation. Yet all the while he was a model to many other married men on board by his constant and knightly courtesy to his own wife.

I have referred elsewhere to the tact of King Edward VII of Great Britain, the most popular sovereign in Europe. This quality is not restricted to public purposes; his acquaintances know that it is untiringly exercised for the benefit of Queen Alexandra, of whose deafness he is never unmindful. Often, when I had the honor to entertain the royal family and their friends, it was my duty to face the King (then Prince of Wales). Sometimes this placed me—embarrassingly too, with my back to the greater part of the audience. But the Prince was regardless of custom and his own royal prerogative, when his consort's enjoyment was endangered; on one occasion when he saw that the Princess was not hearing me distinctly, he said softly to me, "Mr. Wilder, kindly turn your face toward the Princess!"

And Her Royal Highness is as tactful as he. The audience at a special entertainment given the Shah of Persia in London included the most distinguished and wealthy people in the city. I was among those engaged to entertain the Shah, beside whom sat the Princess (now Queen Alexandra). As His Persian Majesty was ignorant of the English language it was not strange that he held his programme upside down. This might have occasioned a laugh and caused the Shah some mortification had not the Princess deftly turned her own programme upside down and kept it so during the performance.

"The Shah held His Program Upside Down."

One of the "nerviest" illustrations of tact is to the credit of Henry Ward Beecher. After the war, he made a lecture tour of the South and appeared at Mozart Hall, Richmond, with an address entitled, "The North and The South." He was rather doubtful as to the reception he would have but he knew what he wanted and was determined to get it. No applause welcomed him as he appeared on the platform, but a few hisses were heard in the gallery. In the better rows of seats were some grim ex-Confederates— General Fitzhugh Lee, General Rosser, ex-Governor Smith, Governor Cameron and others. Beecher fixed his eye directly on Lee and said—(I quote a newspaper report of the incident):

"I have seen pictures of General Fitzhugh Lee, sir, and I assume you are the man. Am I right?"

The General, slightly taken back by this direct address, nodded stiffly, while the audience bent forward, breathless with curiosity as to what was going to follow.

"Then," said Mr. Beecher, his face lighting up, "I want to offer you this right hand, which, in its own way, fought against you and yours, years ago, but which I would now willingly sacrifice to make the sunny South prosperous and happy. Will you take it, General?" There was a moment's hesitation, a moment of deathlike stillness in the hall, and then Fitzhugh

Lee was on his feet, his hand was extended across the footlights and was quickly met by the warm grasp of the preacher's. At first there was a murmur, half of surprise and half of doubtfulness from the audience, then there was a hesitating clapping of hands, and before Beecher had unloosed the hand of Robert E. Lee's nephew, there were cheers such as were never before heard in old Mozart, though it had been the scene of many a war and political meeting. But this was only the beginning of the enthusiasm. When the noise subsided, Mr. Beecher continued,

"When I go back home, I shall proudly tell that I have grasped the hand of the nephew of the great Southern Chieftain; I shall tell my people that I went to the Confederate capital with a heart full of love for the people whom my principles once obliged me to oppose and that I was met halfway by the brave Southerners, who can forgive as well as they can fight."

Five minutes of applause followed, and then, Mr. Beecher, having gained the hearts of his audience, began his lecture and was applauded to the echo. That night, he entered his carriage and drove to his hotel amid shouts such as have never greeted a Northern man in Richmond since the war.

Women who are prominent as hostesses are always remarkable for tact. No matter how they may differ in years, beauty, tastes, nationality, attainments and means, they are classed together by their tact, in the minds of men who know them and know also how arduous are the duties of a successful hostess. I know many such women,—Madame Patti, Mrs. Ronalds, who is one of the most distinguished Americans in London, Mrs. John A. Mackey, the Baroness de Bazus (Mrs. Frank Leslie), Mrs. Kendal—but I could fill a chapter with names. The power of these women in the drawing-room is simply marvelous. Their consummate tact is something for civilization in general to be proud of. It matters not if they are not in their best health and spirits and mood; everything uncongenial in themselves is hidden by their gracious welcome, like Hamlet's father's ghost by the rising sun. In a large company there is likely to be a social knot or tangle that would appal a well meaning novice in the rôle of hostess, but the woman who is fit for the position knows what to ignore and what to illumine.

"There is Apt to Be a Social Tangle."

And cleverness at introductions in a large company—what a world of tact it requires! Small wonder that introductions are few at most fashionable affairs. But the tactful hostess keeps untoward spirits apart and welds congenial souls together; some of the world's closest friendships have come of able hostesses' introductions of people who otherwise would never have met.

But what keen watchfulness and knowledge this presupposes, of the jealousies, petty or large, whether in politics, literature, art, the drama, of a large assemblage of representative people! It requires nothing less than genius to peep into the nooks and crannies of the hearts about them, throbbing with varied purposes and passions, but these women possess it. Hence they are centres in themselves, about which antipathetic souls may gather with a common good-will and cordial good word. It takes all these qualities to be a leader in society: many women possess them, but compared with all who should, how few they are!

I know one woman who possesses them all supremely. She is a wonder, even among Americans. Her name is Mrs. Grover Cleveland. Think of that schoolgirl passing from books to White House receptions and diplomatic balls, from the quick but embarrassed flush of eighteen years, to the sustained, well-poised position of first lady of the land "all in a twinkling" and, more's the wonder, all in a triumph! She went through her ordeal at Washington, for it was an ordeal, without having an enemy in that Babel of bickerings, cunning social plots and desperate plunges after prestige. The platform of the politicians was tariff reform, the people's was Mr. Cleveland, little Ruth, furnishing the "Bye Baby Bunting" plank.

The way this remarkable woman earned love and respect, was illustrated by a little scene, that came under my eye at Lakewood. The parlor of the hotel is so large that men can stand at one end of it with their hats on and escape criticism. But one day, when Mrs. Cleveland, unattended, entered at the other end, with girlish haste and captivating naturalness, all heads were uncovered in an instant. She merely wished to find a friend who was dining at the time, so she walked to the table of her friend. All eyes were upon her, but she manifested no consciousness. She with her friend slipped out of the room and into the elevator, and probably up-stairs for a cozy chat. She was not thinking of the admiring glances of hundreds, but only in a great-hearted, every-day way of her friend. Such is the woman. She has won her crown, woven from the blossoms of the people's love, and she wears it gracefully.

No woman of my acquaintance has more tact than Mrs. Langtry. I will guarantee, that her use of it will win any man who may meet her. When she was last in New York a certain newspaper man was "cutting" her savagely. Did she horsewhip him after the manner of some indignant actress? Nay, nay! First she learned who he was, then she determined to meet him. Her manager invited the young man to dine with him at Delmonico's, and the invitation was accepted. While at dinner the manager accidentally (?) saw Mrs. Langtry, at another table, in the same great dining-room and exclaimed,

"By Jove! There's Mrs. Langtry! Would you like to meet her?" The scribe hesitated; then consented. "First, let me ask her permission," adroitly continued the manager.

"I shall be delighted to meet him," was the lady's reply. Two moments later the scribe and the actress were in close conversation; the young man was invited to Langtry's hotel; he walked down Broadway with her to the Hoffman House, and he knew a thousand men saw him and envied him. In the following week, his paper contained a beautiful article on Langtry. The question may be asked, "Was this tact or diplomacy?" But every one ought to know that mere diplomacy could never make a dramatic critic change his tone so startlingly.

But tact is not confined to incidents in the world's eye. Several years ago, when that clever and beautiful young woman Mrs. James G. Blaine, Jr. (now Mrs. Dr. Bull), was greatly afflicted with rheumatism, her friend, Mrs. Kendal, the well known English actress, advised massage. Mrs. Blaine objected, she disliked the idea, but Mrs. Kendal won her over by calling every day and massaging the sufferer with her own hands.

Men can do the tactful thing as well as women, and it is to their credit that they often do it when they can't imagine that any one will ever know of it but the beneficiary. One rainy day at Broadway and Twenty-third Street, an ill-clad, shivering fellow stood, probably he had nowhere in particular to go, and would rather look at people than think of himself and his condition. I saw a tall, stout man with an intellectual, kind face stop, hold his umbrella over the tramp, and engage him in conversation; it was a mean place to stand, too, for crowds were hurrying past the big policeman standing at the crossing. I dashed in front of the chap the instant the tall man left him.

"See what that man gave me!" he said, showing me a two dollar bill.

"It's no wonder," I replied; "that was Colonel Bob Ingersoll!"

"Hully gee!" the man exclaimed. "I've heard o' him. And here's what else he gave me—listen." The Colonel had told him the story of "Nobody's Dog," as follows:—

"A poor brute of a dog entered a hotel with three travelers. 'Walk in, gents,' said the host heartily. 'Fine dog, that; is he yours, sir?'

"'No,' said one of the men, and 'No,' 'No,' repeated the others.

"I Saw Him Hold His Umbrella Over a Tramp."

"'Then he's nobody's dog,' said the host, as he kicked the cur into the street.

"You're nobody's dog, but here you are," said the Colonel in conclusion, pressing the money into his hand and hurrying away.

I have myself been the gainer by the tact of some men, who would have been excusable for having their minds full of some one of more importance, so I am correspondingly grateful. Dear General Sherman was one of these; his tact was as effective in civil life as his armies had been on the battle-field. In the fall of 1899, just after I had published my book—"The People I Have Smiled With," I received the following written by the General's private secretary.

"MY DEAR SIR:

"I beg you to accept my hearty thanks for a copy of your book, the same which, I assure you, will give me much pleasure in perusing.

"With best wishes, as always, I am,

"Your friend,

(Signed) "W. T. SHERMAN, General."

Evidently the General thought a moment after signing the above, for he wrote at the bottom of the sheet "Over," where he added in his own handwriting:

"Pardon me for this seemingly formal answer to your bright and cheery volume, which, as yet, I have merely glanced at, but contemplate much pleasure and profit in reading. The 'Introduction,' by our mutual friend 'Cockerill,' is so touching that it calls for the sympathetic tear, rather than a smile; so are your opening words in the first chapter about your acquaintance with Beecher, etc., etc. But more in the hereafter.

"I am glad you enroll me in your list of friends, and will be only too happy to smile with you in person over your types, as occasion may require.

"Your sincere friend,

"W. T. SHERMAN."

I might also call attention to the above as an illustration of the occasional opaqueness of the private secretary as a medium between great men and their personal friends, however humble.

I was at Chicago's famous hotel, "The Auditorium" during the dedicatory exercises of the Columbian Exposition, more popularly known as "Chicago's World's Fair." A great dinner had been given the evening before to men distinguished throughout the world. The affair was under the direction of the Fellowship Club, prominent in which was Editor Scott of the Chicago *Herald*, and such a gathering of famous men I had never seen before. Richard Harding Davis described it graphically in *Harper's Weekly*.

Next morning quite naturally, the atmosphere of the hotel was hazy and dazy. Such of us as dropped into the café for breakfast were not especially "noticing."

I sat alone at the end of the room. In came Chauncey M. Depew with a handsome young lady. Before long his quick eye discerned me in my isolation. He arose, walked the entire length of that great room, leaned over me and said,

"Marsh, most through your breakfast?"

"Yes."

"Then come over and be introduced to my niece. She wants to meet the celebrities of the day." Continuing he was kind enough to say that some of my recently delivered jokes were new, and he must have been right, for I heard afterward that he used them himself. But many men of less importance would have sent a waiter for me instead of coming in person; many more would have succeeded in not seeing me at all.

When Mrs. James Brown Potter first visited London, she was chaperoned by Mrs. Paran Stevens, whose daughter, Lady Paget, was a member of the Prince's set, and had full entrée to all social circles. On one occasion Mr. Wilson Barrett set aside a box for Mrs. Stevens, Mrs. Potter, and their friends, I being among the number invited to see "Clito" performed.

In London it is the pleasant custom for the actor-manager to send up refreshments, ices, etc., between the acts, and invite his guests down into his dressing-room. Eccentric Mrs. Stevens hesitated when asked to join us all in going down-stairs to visit Mr. Barrett between the acts. It may have been that she did not wish to incur a social obligation, but whatever the reason, Mrs. Potter, with infinite tact, assumed the rôle of charmed and charming guest, allowing Mrs. Stevens to remain quietly unobserved and free from any future embarrassment.

Mme. Nordica displayed her charming tactfulness one Sunday at a musicale given by Mrs. Ronalds in London. It was when peace was declared between England and the Boers. The news arrived about 4 P. M. Instantly Mme. Nordica sprang to her feet, and sang "God Save the King." It was most inspiring, coming just as it did, and those who were present will never forget how the people stood about clapping their hands and rejoicing over this great event, which was announced by an American.

XX
ADELINA PATTI

Her home in Wales.—Some of Her Pets.—An Ocean Voyage With Her.—The Local Reception at Her Home-Coming.—Mistress of an Enormous Castle and a Great Retinue of Servants.—Her Winter Garden and Private Theatre.—A Most Hospitable and Charming Hostess.—Her Local Charities Are Continuous and Many.

Craig-y-Nos (Craig-of-the-Night) in the Swansea Valley, Ystradgnlais, South Wales, by river and meadow and mountain, is the home of Madame Patti.

Among madame's pets at her castle is one Jumbo, an American parrot, who carried with him to Wales his country's admiration for his mistress. For when she goes forth into the great world, he puts on a dejected bearing, and in a voice touched with tears keeps calling, "Where is Patti? Where is Patti?" But the parrot only gives word to what is felt by all the good folks of Swansea Valley; for the pets and the people, of high and low degree, miss this wonderful little woman when she is away, and she in turn longs for her pets and her peasants, her country roads and princely retreat, with that whole-hearted longing which doubtless gives much to the depth of feeling the world knows in her rendition of "Home, Sweet Home." This little song, that makes the whole world kin, bears to the difficult song work of Patti some such relation as does her life of artlessness to her life of art. Her nature undisguised is childlike and spontaneous.

When I took ship on the *City of New York* in May, 1892, in the same party with Madame Patti, and her husband, Signor Nicolini, she was full of greetings, and words of parting to those coming and going just before we sailed.

Nicolini's devotion to his wife was the remark of the ship. He was ever thoughtful of her, and his services were continual, from his first one in the morning, that of delivering her mail to her.

Previous to sailing, a Boston lady friend had sent aboard seven or eight letters, with the direction that one should each morning be delivered to Madame Patti. What a merrymaking there was when the usual, or rather, unusual letter bobbed up every morning! A fresh-cheeked young country girl could not have been more demonstrative. But such is her single-mindedness: her heart is young, and that is no doubt one of the great causes of the depth of her beauty. An ocean voyage generally washes out the skin-deep variety, but when I saw Patti every day, rich Spanish beauty turned up with her every time. She was the pet of the people without seeming to be conscious of it, and went along through the days like other folks, speaking to friend after friend in the language of their preference, for it makes no difference to her—German, French, Spanish, Italian or English; and with all her naïvete, she is an adroit and charming diplomat.

"You must visit me," she said one day on the steamer to me. "I will not take no for an answer. I will follow you all over England with telegrams, if you do not."

"I will follow you all over England with telegrams."

I went.

At Paddington station I found that my hostess was truly a royal one, for there was the private car of His Royal Highness, the Prince of Wales, awaiting her. The interior was banked with flowers, from end to end, and snatching up bunches here and there, Patti would be all in a glee over them. As the train moved, three beautiful young girls ran down the length of the station to get a last glimpse of Patti. Two of them threw up their hands, their faces flushed with the race; but the third sped to the end of the platform. It was a pretty picture.

In our party were Madame and Monsieur Nicolini, madame's companion and two maids, Nicolini's attendant and valet. I completed the group, and with reason was congratulating myself, knowing the scarcity and luxury of the private car in England. As we swept by Neath, the former home of my hostess, then the seat of Henry M. Stanley, her eyes sparkled, for home meant so much to her, and she was almost there. What a lark there was too on our short run, with Patti singing "On the Bowery," and snatches from other "fad" airs, Nicolini joining in, and now breaking away on his own account into "Annie Rooney" with the refrain, "Adelina Patti is my sweetheart."

We were met at the station by a corps of servants, a big drag, and equipages for guests, and were driven in handsome style around the frowning brow of the great craig, into full view of the castle, spreading out its arms as if in gladness at the happy home-coming of its queen.

As we neared the great gate all the household gathered to meet us, from the head man Heck, to the stable boys. It seemed to me that I had been assigned to the choice of the eighty rooms of the castle, so luxurious were all the appointments about me.

"The clever bird surprised me by ejaculating Pity Patti."

I spoke of the pets. There were twenty-five or thirty varieties of birds, besides donkeys, ponies and rare dogs, of which Patti is very fond, always having numbers of them accompany her in her walks. Ten of these birds were parrots. Each one of these birds had acquired that peculiar style of eloquence best suited to his disposition and temperament. For example, one day when Patti got a trifling hurt, the clever bird surprised me by ejaculating, "Pity Patti!" This gushing bird has ever since maintained a steady sympathy, spending most of his verbally unhappy life saying "Pity Patti! Pity Patti!" As you go up to each parrot, he thus, with some different speech unburdens his mind to you. They are sociable birds, spending most of their time together, and when, new and then, a sewing-society notion strikes them all at once, it might be called a unanimous change of subject.

From the moment of arrival, a valet is put at the service of the guest, and orders are taken by him at night, for the following morning's breakfast.

There is no rising time. While Patti is an early riser, she makes no such demands upon her guests. The valet appears at the hour ordered, prepares the bath, and serves breakfast at any time desired. Patti after her regular morning bath, takes her breakfast, and reads her daily mail before going out for the day. The guest is absolutely free to do as he wishes until half-past twelve. During my morning strolls I often met Patti sauntering through the grounds with her well-beloved dogs.

At half-past twelve all meet at luncheon, and all must be prompt. At this little *déjeuner*, which is by no means a light meal, Patti is a gale of joyous chat and greeting. The trivial incident is touched into color by her vitality.

Then comes the famous afternoon drive. As a rule the homes of the neighborhood are connected by telephone with the castle, and invitations come and go. One afternoon we drove to a farmhouse of a neighbor, where we saw a contest between three sheep dogs. There were three sheep to each dog, and that one was proclaimed winner who most quickly drove his three sheep through one opening into a corral. It was an intensely interesting illustration of the instinctive sheep-driving skill of the dogs. Then again we would go for a long spin over the hills through the keen mountain air.

A light English tea at five, after which we had until half-past seven to rest and dress before appearing at dinner, the great event of the day. All, of course, wear full dress, gathering in the boudoir where one sees pictures and autographs of famous people the world over. Among the photographs I noticed those of Mrs. Cleveland, Christine Nilsson, Nieman, Albani, Scalchi, Hans Richter, Verdi, and the King and Queen of Italy. A full length portrait of Mrs. Cleveland appears beside that of the Princess of Wales. The coloring, hangings, and wall coverings are all suggestive of restfulness in their richness.

The first announcement one has of dinner is a melody of silver bells. The notes seem to cling to the bells until they are fairly shaken off like bubbles into the air; then there seem to be two melodies, one the tender musical shadow of the other.

Nicolini would go in front of madame, who quickly took his arm and they would lead the way into the great conservatory or winter garden, where flowers are rushing into bloom the year round. The fragrant air is musical with singing birds, and the effect is magical under the effulgence of the electroliers. The windows command a magnificent view of the country around, mountain and valley and winding river, spread just at the feet of the castle; salmon brooks, stretches of thousands of acres, and hunting grounds covering nearly ten miles of fine shooting. With her own fingers Patti puts a boutonnière on guests here and there, and then we intrust ourselves to the mercy of one of Britain's greatest chefs.

Just here I am reminded of Norris, the Irish butler, whose sense of humor almost broke up his self-possession. At the table while I was telling stories he would hold down his upper lip with his teeth, like the side of a tent, afraid to let it go, lest it might be blown away by a breeze of laughter. As it was, the lip kept wrinkling. Both Madame Patti and I saw it, but concealed our knowledge from Norris, for the poor conventional soul's heart would have been broken, had he suspected that we knew of his having lost the icy calm of a properly conducted butler. He would "list" his head over to one side, cough, fly around in unnecessary ways, and altogether expend a great deal of energy in keeping down the humorous side of his nature.

The attachment of Patti's servants to her is as constant as that of her friends and her pets. Norris had been with her thirteen years; one servant had been with her five years; another, her Swedish valet, for nine years; then there were the driver, Joe; George, her courier; and the general manager, a man of varied accomplishments and great executive ability, Guillaume Heck.

Among all those about her, none is so close as is Caroline Baumeister, an Austrian woman, her companion, who has been with her nearly forty years. Constantly at her side with her council and care, Caroline is Patti's friend in every sense of the word. Of excellent family, robust in mind and body, of that well-balanced, soothing and serene temperament which has finally made Patti a child in her dependence upon it. Caroline has a Mexican girl, Padro, as her assistant.

After dinner we pass into the billiard rooms, of which there are two, with French and English and American tables. At the end of one of these rooms is a monster orchestrion, which cost thirty thousand dollars, and which furnishes music during the games. Anything may be played on it, from Wagner to the latest popular air, by simply inserting a roll. These rolls, by the way, cost one hundred dollars each; in truth golden music.

During these little after-dinner billiard games the sincerity and simplicity of Patti is seen to great advantage. For instance, imagine the picture of the great diva catching up a billiard cue, and marching around the room, followed by all the guests, to the tune of the Turkish March played on the orchestrion. Often during the course of the evening, when she could stand the buoyant effect of the music no longer, she would break into song, trilling as naturally as a bird, and as spontaneously.

After a certain time spent in the billiard rooms, we would wander through a continuation of the winter garden, into one of the most cherished possessions of Patti, her private theatre. This theatre was erected at a great cost, and with a care for detail which may be imagined, when it is known that Mr. Irving sent down his head carpenter from London, to see that perfection was reached at every point. Mr. Irving has said several times that it was the most perfect thing of its kind he had ever seen. Every property is complete; there are the traps, the thunder and lightning, everything metropolitan, even the floor, which is adjustable either for inclined auditorium purposes or for the level of a ball-room floor. There are six dressing-rooms, and the stage, built for sixty people, has a "run" of eighty feet, while the auditorium will accommodate three hundred and fifty and the gallery eighty people. During the little evenings, the gallery is generally filled by domestics and peasants. Programmes are prepared with elegance for each entertainment. I have one now—the operatic matinée in honor of His Royal Highness, Prince Henry of Battenberg, and party:

Overture "Martha," orchestra. Vocal concert (artists, Madame Adelina Patti-Nicolini, Madame Giulia Valda, Signor Vovara), "Faust" Act III, Garden Scene, in which Signor Nicolini, as Faust, took part. The conductor was Signor Arditi. The programme is richly embellished in purple and scarlet and gold.

One of the ornaments on the walls of this beautiful little theatre is the armor worn by Patti in her creation, at the age of nineteen, of the character of Joan of Arc. She also appears in a splendid painting on the curtain, as "Semiramis" in her triumphal car.

During my stay the idea struck Patti of having a little entertainment in my honor. So George, the courier, was posted off to Swansea to get an orchestra, and other parts of the equipment needed for this hasty-pudding matinée, for there was only one day in which to get ready.

It took place June 15th, 1892. The programme was filled by Patti and four or five friends, including myself in the humorous number. Patti's voice can never be heard to such advantage as under the shadow of her mountains in this peaceful valley; here she sings from very gladness because she is free. She is out of the cage (for Patti is never so caged as when before the public) in her own home where song is not an article of merchandise, but the gratuitous offering of nature. So it is that her trills are more brilliant and spontaneous than the same flights for which she receives five thousand dollars a night.

Every Christmas a thousand children are entertained, and a charity concert is given, when presents are distributed by her to the poor of Swansea and Neath districts, being handed out by her personally.

Her good offices to the poor are done in numberless ways, the greater part unknown. I heard during my visit this story: there was a poor child born just inside the big gate one evening. The quivering peasant mother, homeless and alone, turned instinctively in her agony to the good mistress of the valley, and had crawled within the friendly shelter of the lady's wall. Patti, returning from a drive found them and took them to her home and had them cared for. She named the little tot Craig-y-Nos. When all was well, the woman offered to work out the debt, but "No," said her hostess, "you are my guests."

There is a standing rule that no poor shall be turned away from the castle. Each one, no matter how deserving, is given bread and beer, and they come in continually from miles around.

"Lady of the Castle," she is affectionately called by the plain folk of that country. Can one wonder then that when she drives out all greet her with grateful deference, and the little children curtsey as if to a queen. Whenever I drove out with her I saw the same demonstration.

Patti has a retinue of sixty domestics while she is at home, and leaves twenty-five to look after things when she is away. There is a complete electric plant with a power-house so far away as to avoid the noise of the machinery; also a gas plant, if this light is preferred; a telephone and telegraph service connect the castle with the outside world. Let me not forget the dairy, the steam laundry, and the refrigerating facilities for the meats. The stables are elegantly constructed and equipped, there being seven pairs of carriage horses beside the riding horses, ponies and donkeys.

One of the ponies had been pensioned after long and faithful service, and spent most of his time browsing in the paddock with Jenny, the little pet donkey of the place. The two were uncommonly knowing and the fastest of friends, one running in front of a person trying to catch the other. This manœuvre they could successfully carry out, until the one trying to catch either of them would retire in disgust, to the great satisfaction of Tom and Jenny, who would peacefully resume their tête-à-tête meal.

With all the paraphernalia of comfort and convenience, it remains only for the personality of Patti to convert the castle into home. What a hostess! During my stay everything seemed to be done with special reference to me. Even the American flag was hoisted on the castle in honor of my nationality. Thus special guests are always flatteringly recognized by the sight of their own country's flag. The individual tastes of the guests are studied to the minutest degree by all. For instance, I have always been very fond of ice. Imagine this trifling taste of mine being detected without my knowledge. I found out that it had been in this way. When I left I found my lunch providently and daintily put up, and among the delicacies I discovered a piece of ice! It had been frozen into a small block specially for me, and I enjoyed it very much, all the trip.

Then again, I had expressed an interest in her jewels, so during my stay she decked herself every night with different ones, all in my honor, as she assured me.

Do what she will, this woman, worshiped of all nations, is the willing slave of a loving heart. Her old parents, whom she loved and revered when they were living, she loves and honors now that they are dead, and not a day passes, without some fond reference to them.

A friend of Patti's, a French lady, met with distressing financial losses. In her need Patti said to her, "Come and live with me!" and she did, for many happy years after that.

When Joe was driving me to Penwyllt I thought of it all as the road lengthened between me and my friends. I remembered that Patti had told me that of all American cities, Richmond and Syracuse were her favorites, but I feel sure she is the favorite of all our cities.

The world has been made glad by her song, but not more glad than the mountain district by her presence. There she lives a queen, crowned by the love of all about her.

XXI
SOME NOTABLE PEOPLE

Cornelius Vanderbilt.—Mrs. Mackey.—The Rockefellers.—Jay Gould.—George Gould and Mrs. Edith Kingdom Gould.—Mary Anderson.—Mrs. Minnie Maddern Fiske.—Augustin Daly.—Nicola Tesla.—Cheiro.

The mass of the people envy most the men and women who have most money; my own envy goes out hungrily to those who are happiest, though I have sometimes inclined strongly toward the majority. One day in London, while my mind was full of the good that a great lot of money would do me, I learned that Mr. Cornelius Vanderbilt, who was still suffering from the effects of a paralytic stroke, was at a hotel in Piccadilly. Besides being one of the best men in the world, he had been one of my best friends, so I called on him, hoping I might cheer his heart in some way and make him forget his trouble. It was hard to get at him, for his secretary had been ordered by the physician to admit no one, but I got my card to him, and he was kind enough to express a wish to see me and a belief that my visit would do him good.

From Mr. Vanderbilt's hotel I went to the home of Mrs. John A. Mackey, whose son Willie had recently lost his life by being thrown from his horse. I had no desire to intrude upon grief, but Willie and I had been merry friends together, and I believed remembrance of our acquaintance would make Mrs. Mackey willing to see me. Here again I had great difficulty; the butler had received positive order, and it took me twenty minutes to persuade him that Mrs. Mackey would not refuse to receive my card. I was right, for she was very glad to see me. Her house was a veritable palace, containing everything valuable and artistic that money would buy, yet amid all these evidences of wealth the bereaved mother sat in deep black, mourning the loss of her beloved son and, like Rachel, "would not be comforted." So my visits to these two good friends convinced me that money could not do everything.

Probably the most envied man in America is John D. Rockefeller, for his income alone is believed to exceed half a million dollars a day. There are many men and women near Owego, N. Y., who attended school with John Rockefeller, in the little schoolhouse on the old river road. They did not regard him as a prospective millionaire: he was merely "one of the Rockefeller boys," yet they knew him from the first as the leader of boys of his age. He was the first to suggest a game of sport, and those who remember him best assert that unless John had his own way he would not play. He did not fly into a rage when opposed and overruled, but he would watch the play without taking part in it. And such has been his business policy; it is a matter of record that he has embarked in no business ventures not of his own suggestion, nor in any of which he had not full control.

Like another great financier, Jay Gould, his personality dominated every undertaking in which he was interested; neither he nor Gould allowed any one to think for them. Both men were alike in another respect; they brought up their sons in the same self-reliant manner, instead of allowing them to drop into luxury and self-indulgence, after the manner of most millionaires' sons.

Young Mr. Rockefeller is a man of simple and regular habits, but not at all afraid to enter the field of labor in competition with great brain-workers. He is a creditable exponent of his father's business creed.

Jay Gould once wrote as follows, in a letter to a personal friend:

"Man seems to be so constituted that he cannot comprehend his own situation. To-day he lends his ear to the charming words of the deceiver and is led to believe himself a god; to-morrow he is hissed and laughed at for some fancied fault, and, rejected and broken-hearted, he retires to his chamber to spend a night in tears. These are certainly unwarranted positions: the first to ingratiate himself or obtain your notice, and therefore his delusion of greatness is unwarranted, while the latter is the voice of the envious—those who look with a war-like spirit upon the tide of your prosperity, since they deem themselves equally meritorious. And this last assumption, over which you have shed your tears, is the true voice of your praise!"

"Luxury and self-indulgence after the manner of most millionaire sons."

Only the man who had thus accurately gauged the world's estimate of wealthy men could have been the example and inspiration of George Gould, upon whose shoulders was laid a burden of almost incalculable weight, which he has borne successfully and without making a public show of himself and his millions. He is a genuine man, and has a worthy companion in his wife, who as a bride went from the stage to the home of one of the wealthiest young men in the land, yet whose admirable womanhood has never been marred by consciousness of great riches. She has never forgotten her old professional associates whom she liked, nor, indeed, any mere acquaintance. Not long ago she happened to see me in the studio of Marceau, the photographer. Leaving some friends with whom she had been conversing she came over to me, greeted me cordially, and congratulated me heartily on my marriage, yet with the unstudied simplicity and directness for which she is noted.

Early in life I became an autograph hunter and an admirer of stage deities of both sexes, and one of the first autographs I ever got was that of Mary Anderson, who gave it very graciously. Since then she has favored me with others, but that first one is among my dearest treasures. The American people were in accord with me in admiration of Miss Anderson. She was lovingly referred to as "Our Mary" and her success in this country was regarded as a guarantee of an enthusiastic reception abroad.

But the English public is hard to approach; to please on this side of the water is not an assurance of success over there, and Miss Anderson's appearance did not make an exception to the rule. For sometimes she had poor audiences at the Lyceum (London). Efforts were made to have the Prince of Wales attend a performance, but for a time they were unsuccessful. One night he entered the theatre and was so much pleased that after the first act he sent word to the stage that he wished to see Miss Anderson. The lady's mother, Mrs. Griffen, who received his message, requested that he would defer the meeting until the end of the play, as she feared the honor might "upset" her daughter and mar the performance. The Prince replied: "Certainly," like the considerate gentleman he always is.

Meanwhile Michael Gunn, the manager of the theatre, with characteristic managerial shrewdness, saw a great chance for advertising, so he rushed off by a cable to America a message which read:

"Mary Anderson refuses to see the Prince of Wales without the Princess."

The difference in time—five hours, between the two countries gave him the advantage he wanted. The New York papers got it barely in time for their last editions. Next day they cabled London papers for particulars, but the day of a great American morning paper does not begin until noon or later, by which time, say 6 P. M. on the other side of the Atlantic, all London is at dinner or getting ready for it and must not be disturbed. Besides, the English papers do not exhibit American taste and enterprise in nosing out news. So they published the story as a fact, and without comment. It was too small a matter for either of the parties to formally deny in print, but it was large enough to make no end of talk and of interest in the American actress. From that bit of advertising shrewdness—some Englishmen gave it a ruder name, dated Miss Anderson's success in London.

Mention of Miss Anderson recalls a reception in her honor which I attended, at the home of Mrs. Croly ("Jennie June"). Among the guests was a young actress who was just coming into notice—Miss Minnie Maddern, now Mrs. Fiske. Her beautiful, expressive eyes followed the guest of honor so wistfully that I said:

"I see you are observing Miss Anderson intently."

"Yes," she replied. "What a beautiful woman she is! And what an actress! What wouldn't I give to be able to act as she can!"

Such modesty has its reward. Mrs. Fiske has not only reached the plane of Mary Anderson's ability, but has gone far above it, and stands to-day upon a pinnacle of art that no other American actress has ever climbed. One night, at a performance of "Hedda Gabler," I asked my friend Charles Kent, whose high rank as an actor is admitted by every one, if Mrs. Fiske was not our greatest actress. He replied:

"Mrs. Fiske is more than our greatest actress She is the greatest personality in the profession. She is the Henry Irving of America."

One of the greatest losses the American stage ever sustained was through the death of Augustin Daly. I have heard some of his most determined rivals call him the greatest stage manager in America, and since his death they have expressed doubt that his equal would ever appear. I was his neighbor for quite a while; I saw him often and chatted much with him, but I never knew a man less given to "talking shop." Apparently he had no thought for anything but his two sons, both of whom were then living, and on Sunday mornings it was a great pleasure to me to see him walking with his boys to the Catholic Church, of which he was a devout member. But he lost both sons in a single week, one dying, broken-hearted, after the death of the other. The double loss was one from which Mr. Daly never recovered, though he sought relief in hard work. I often met him after midnight on the old green car that passed through Thirty-fourth Street, yet next morning saw him leave the house as early as eight o'clock. Busy though he was, he never forgot his friends; he was so kind as to keep them under continual obligations. I recall a complimentary dinner which Major Handy wished to give Mr. Daly, but when he approached the prospective guest, Daly said:

"Oh, you invite your friends, and I'll give the dinner."

New York managers are seldom visible in the front of the house during a performance, but Mr. Daly's eyes seemed to be there as well as on the stage. At the hundredth performance of "The Taming of the Shrew" the house was packed; after endeavoring in vain to buy a seat I stood at the railing, where Mr. Daly saw me and said:

"Come with me, Marsh."

We went up-stairs to the balcony where he got a camp-stool from somewhere and placed it for me in the middle aisle, whispering me at the same time to fold it at the end of the performance and bring it down to him, as he was breaking one of the ordinances regarding fires in theatres by allowing me to sit in the aisle.

Dr. Nicola Tesla, the great electrician, is an oft-seen figure, yet his retiring disposition and his distaste for society make him personally unknown. Any one who has visited the Waldorf in the evening must have seen this interesting man sitting alone at a table in a corner of the winter garden, for there he is, night after night, after his solitary dinner, wrapped in his thoughts. He has told me that here, in an atmosphere of bustle and chatter, he can think better than anywhere else: he is oblivious to the people who stare curiously at him, for his mind is absorbed in the details of some wonderful invention. He lives at the Waldorf; once he thought of leaving, so he packed his trunks. His departure was postponed from day to day, so his trunks remained unopened: rather than unpack them he purchased new things from time to time according to his necessities. Finally he decided to remain at the Waldorf, but for all I know to the contrary the trunks still remain unpacked.

I have the honor of being numbered among Dr. Tesla's friends, so I have often stopped at his table for a chat, but never without his invitation. Most sensitive natures are so self-absorbed as to be utterly selfish, but Dr. Tesla, although sensitive in the extreme, is always considerate of the feelings of others. I know of many occasions on which he displayed this rare quality, and I may be pardoned for mentioning one which concerned myself. I sent Dr. Tesla a copy of my book "People I've Smiled With" and received a polite acknowledgment, which was followed almost immediately by a long letter, as if he feared I had been hurt by the shortness of the earlier communication.

"He was reading a lady's palm."

Several of my friends were at the Victoria Hotel in London while I was also stopping there, and among them was Miss Loie Fuller, who usually held an informal reception after theatre hours—the Thespian's only "recess." One evening, on returning from an entertainment I had given, I went into Miss Fuller's parlor and found the hostess and her friends clustered about a gentleman whom I did not know. He had dark hair and eyes and was extremely good looking—a perfect type of Irish manhood. He was reading a lady's palm, and the others were listening with great interest. Soon Miss Fuller said:

"I want you to read Marshall's palm."

"Oh, yes," said the others; "let's hear what Marshall's luck will be."

We were introduced; his name was Louis Warner, and on looking at my hand he began to tell my characteristics with an accuracy which was startling. I had no opportunity for conversation with him that evening, so I invited him to lunch with me the next day. He came and we had a very interesting chat about palmistry. I asked him if he made a business of it and he said he did not—he was an actor, and playing at the Princess Theatre.

"Do you ever think of taking up palmistry as a business?" I asked.

"No," he answered, "but I may some day."

I told him I thought there was a great deal of money in it, to which he assented. During the conversation he kept calling me Mr. Marshall; when I corrected his mistake and told him what my name was, he was much surprised, and asked my pardon for making the mistake. I told him I was glad he had, for it showed me more clearly the truth of his palmistry.

"Of course I know you by reputation," he said. "You did a great deal for Heron-Allen in America, helping him to get acquainted there."

"Yes," I replied, "and if you ever come over there I'll do what I can to introduce you."

A year later I was walking through the corridor of the Imperial Hotel (New York) when I was stopped by a gentleman, who said:

"You don't remember me, do you, Mr. Wilder?"

"Yes," I answered, "you are Louis Warner of London." He laughed and said:

"You have a very good memory, Mr. Wilder, but I have taken another name. I wish to be known as Cheiro. I have chosen that name as it is the Greek word for 'hand,' and while appropriate it is also an attractive one for professional work. You see, I have followed your advice, and taken up palmistry as a business."

I introduced him to a great many of my friends, and he was most successful in reading their palms correctly. A little later, a lady called upon me, asking me to give her topics for newspaper work. I gave her some letters to friends of mine,—well known men, asking them to let her take an impression of their hands. She visited, among others, Mr. Russell Sage, Mr. Chauncey Depew and Sir Henry Irving, who was in town, taking impressions of their hands on paper with printer's ink. She also entered the Tombs and obtained the impression of the hand of a notorious forger. These she took to Cheiro, and without knowing whose hands they were he read each and every one correctly. Among them was an impression of my own hand. He picked it up, and said immediately:

"This is the hand of my friend, Marshall Wilder." To my mind, this was the greatest test of his powers.

The story was written up, readily sold to a newspaper, and was copied many times, widely read and commented upon. Since then Cheiro's work has become known all over the world.

XXII
HUMAN NATURE

Magnetism and Its Elements.—Every one Carries the Marks of His Trade.—How Men are "Sized Up" at Hotels.—Facial Resemblance of Some People to Animals.—What the Eye First Catches.—When Faces are Masked.—Bathing in Japan.—The Conventions in Every-Day Life that Hide Us from Our Fellows.—Genuineness is the One Thing Needful.

The oftener a man—any man, from the beginner at vaudeville to the great actor or orator—appears before audiences, the more he is impressed by the many varieties of human nature and the many ways there are of comprehending it.

A few people who have to meet large numbers of their fellow-beings have no trouble on this score, for they possess something that for lack of a better name is called magnetism. Some actors who are full of faults succeed by means of this quality; twenty times as many who are more intelligent and thorough fail through lack of it. The same may be said of Congressmen, lawyers, preachers and presidents. Magnetism seems to be a combination of sensitiveness, affection, impulse and passion, so it is not strange that only a few people of any profession possess it.

For instance, go into Weber & Fields when both Lillian Russell and Fay Templeton are on the bill. The former delights the eye and ear, for she is beautiful with a charming voice. Yet Miss Templeton gets beyond the eye and ear to the heart; she takes possession of the company as well as of the audience; even the "chorus"—and the chorus is noted for paying no attention to anything or anybody but itself and its personal friends—loves Fay Templeton and manifests close interest in her work.

But one need not be on the stage to study human nature. Wherever there is a successful business organization, there you will find close observers of human nature. Go into a great hotel—the Astoria for instance—and even the bell-boys are adepts to it. Walk down the lobby, supposing yourself unobserved, and you are "sized up" at once. If you are a reporter, the whole house from the bell-boys to the head clerk know that you are not of a class that can be "pigeon-holed." The Southern man, with his family on a pleasure jaunt, is accurately "tabbed" at once. So is the public man—not always by his clothes, but by his manner. The "drummer" signifies his business by a side-to-side movement, something like a wheat-hopper in an elevator. The prominent man betrays himself by using his legs as if they were intended solely to hold up his body, which, no matter how well off he may be, is almost sure to have an empty buttonhole somewhere. The needy man is likely to be carefully clad, but his trousers are out of season, a trifle short and pieced out with gaiters. The hotel clerk takes in all these signs at a glance, and gives answers and rooms accordingly.

"The needy man is likely to be carefully clad."

I believe many men size up people by resemblances to animals; I know I do, and with uniform success—when I select the right animal; so my mind contains a menagerie of acquaintances and a few strangers not yet identified. It is almost impossible to see a man with a fox-face without finding him foxy. Then there are monkey faces, with eyes close together and shifty—eyes that seem to look into each other. Beware of them! I have heard good housekeepers say that they prefer servants with eyes wide apart, for the other kind have invariably been connected with missing silver and other portable property. Nearly every criminal whose portrait appears in the "Rogues' Gallery" has monkey eyes; the criminal class is recruited from this type.

The bulldog face may be seen every day among the never-give-up men in every business. The late William M. Evarts' face suggested the eagle, and he made some great fights side by side with our national bird. What is the matter with Joseph H. Choate as the owl, the late Recorder Smyth as the hawk, Dr. Parkhurst as the wary tabby on watch for the mouse? We have some orators who look like pug-dogs; preachers who resemble fashionably sheared poodles, and I know one unmistakable Dachshund of the pulpit. Strong combinations are occasionally seen; Roger A. Pryor suggests a cleancut greyhound with the face of a mastiff. Other men resemble great-hearted St. Bernards, with intelligent eyes and a reserve force that is never squandered on trifles or bickerings. Daily, one may see a man in a carriage with his dog, and the two look so alike that you hesitate to say which dog is driving.

The first thing apt to be noticed about a man is his hat; then his shoes, collar and clothes in the order named; the face is generally left to the last, though it should be the first. Nothing is so significant to me as the eye, especially if it won't look straight at me. Some men of great mental vitality carry so much strength focalized in the eye that they absolutely absorb. After an earnest conversation with such a person one feels as if he had done a day's work.

"You hesitate to say which dog is driving."

Men often suggest their business occupations by their walk. A dentist displays the gait and bearing he has when he is coming to the side of your chair to draw a tooth. A printer carries his arm forward, as if feeling for the "case." The preacher you can almost hear saying "Now we will hear from Brother Hawkins." The rôles of stage people stick to them on the outside; the tragedian I rarely mistake; the "leading man" can't get rid of his descriptive look. The villain and the comedian you will know apart, although, strange to say, their real characters are generally diametrically opposite to the parts they play.

Faces are like looking-glasses; they generally reflect the treatment they receive. Driving in the park, the wealthy lady wants Mrs. Jones to know she is on deck—footman, mountings, dog-chairs and all. You can tell her by the "Oh-have-I-to-go-through-with-this-again?" sort of look. The young Wall Street plunger's face says, "You thought I wouldn't be here, eh? well, here I am." One man's face tells you he is driving with his sweetheart; the simple soft quietude of one woman's face tells you that she is beyond all else a mother.

As a rule, however,—and more's the pity—a man's real nature is obscured when he is in pursuit of gain—absorbed in business, of any kind. You would no more know him then, than you would your own house-cat when the Mr. Hyde side of his nature crops out on your garden fence late at night. Two boys were selling newspapers on a car; the larger in his eagerness for business, pushed the other off. The little fellow fell, dropped and scattered his papers and began to cry. Instantly the big boy was a different being; he lost all thought of business, hurried to his disabled rival, put the little chap on his feet and got his papers together for him.

Some people have a magnetic manner that is both instant and quelling in its effect. A certain woman enters a parlor, and for some subtle, indefinable reason all eyes are fixed upon her. She may not be brilliant yet she holds the winning hand; she bears on her face "a royal flush," yet let her go out and some inferior will say, "now that she's gone, we can talk about her." Her quality is generally called instinctive, but probably it was slowly acquired, for lives are like lead-pencils—it takes long experience to sharpen them so they will leave a clear, keen line. Sometimes this line appears in the profile, which I have often believed a sure indication of character; so did Talleyrand.

Human expression is much affected by geographical location and custom. An American in Japan asked his host's servants for a bath, and was soon informed it was ready. As he saw nothing to indicate its whereabouts, he asked,

"Where?"

"Look out into the garden, sir." He looked and saw his hostess and host, the latter being governor of the town, awaiting him, beside an artificial pool, and entirely nude. He was told that according to Japanese custom the first plunge is the right of the guest, so there was no time to lose, for the good people were shivering while they waited. The guest went out looking like Adam before the downfall, and much embarrassed besides. Stepping into the water he found it too hot and begged for cold water; the Japanese take only warm baths, but at once the pool was emptied and cold water was turned in. Meanwhile the lord and lady stood as unadorned as Greek statues, this being Japanese custom while waiting at a bath. Such a performance in New York would cause even Tammany to rally around Dr. Parkhurst, but in Japan it "goes." This gentle, courteous, considerate family also expressed wonder at the straightness of their guest's legs, their own being bent through the habit of sitting on them in tailor-fashion;—Japanese custom again.

When men do not act in accordance with their looks, some tradition or custom of their ancestors or associates will account for it; a man is generally a Democrat because his father was one, though it doesn't invariably follow that because "the governor" is a total abstainer the "Martigny" is unknown to his son. Men unconsciously initiate other men and their ways, because other men have done it. We dress in black when some one dear to us dies.

Why, oh men of Athens, do we do these things? Should any dear relative of mine die, I think I would go to the theatre that night,—if I felt like it. I believe, with Mr. Beecher, in rose-colored funerals; not in those which are gray and ghostly with ashes. There is too much convention about these things. Why do we have all the formal funerals, when the only real sentiment is attended to by the hearts of the bereaved? When the body is dead it should be put away quietly, kindly, reverently, but without any display of tears—and without the cards and flowers. They are the style, you know, but—why cards? Why shouldn't we send flowers anonymously, so as to spare the real mourners the pains of writing an acknowledgment? Let us steer clear of conventional sorrow when we can, for there is enough of the real article to go round. If the night must come, sprinkle it with stars; if there be the winding sheet of snow, tinkle sleigh bells over it. The living want your love far more than the dead want your tears.

But, after all that can and must be said against it, human nature is kind. Deceit, love of gain, suspicion and even violence are often mere means of defense. Get through the joints of any one's every-day armor and reach the heart and the same sweet response of sympathy rings out, the world over, in tones as mellow as old Trinity's chimes on New Year's eve, and self-disguised people become genuine. For illustration, let an old man or old woman enter a streetcar crowded with men whose faces are hard with business cares; why every seat is at their disposal; there is the genuineness of the people.

Yet if we were all and always genuine there would be no human nature to study, for "Truth is simple, requiring neither study nor art."

XXIII
SUNNY STAGE PEOPLE

"Joe" Jefferson.—I Take His Life.—His Absent-Mindedness.—Jefferson and General Grant.—Nat Goodwin and How He Helped Me Make Trouble.—Our Bicycling Mishap.—Goodwin Pours Oil on Troubled Dramatic Waters Abroad.—George Leslie.—Wilton Lackaye.—Burr McIntosh.—Miss Ada Rehan.

Every class of people on earth contains a pleasing number of cheery folk, but far the greatest proportion is found in the theatrical profession. Get together, if you can, all the companionable, hospitable souls of all other classes and the stage people by themselves can make almost as good a showing. When talking of them I never know where to begin or how to stop, for they have loaded me with kindnesses, and began it when I was on the extreme outer edge of a profession which they regarded as a mere side show to their own.

Years ago when I was on the lecture platform I used to have some cloudy hours, in spite of my efforts to be sunny, for, unlike theatrical people, lecturers are usually their own only traveling companions, the railway runs are long, the engagements are what the dramatic agents call "one night stands," so the stops are so short that the lecturer has no chance to adapt his digestive apparatus to the surprises that unknown chefs of unknown hotels delight in springing upon him. Years ago—as I said a moment ago, I was thinking of all these miseries, as I left a train at Utica on a snowy, stormy afternoon of the Christmas holidays, when I specially longed to be with some friends in New York. I had four blank hours before me, for I was not to appear on the platform until evening, and it was one of the days when I was too tired to study or read and too shaken up to sleep. Suddenly a negro porter in drawing-room car uniform accosted me with:

"Mr. Wilder, Mr. Jefferson would like to see you."

He pointed to the right, and there in the window of a parlor car, sidetracked for the day only, stood "Joe" Jefferson. When I got into the car and looked about me I saw the great "all-star" cast of "The Rivals"—dear Mme. Ponisi, Mr. John Drew, Viola Allen, W. J. Florence, Otis Skinner, Frederic Paulding, Frank Bangs, George Dunham, Elsie C. Lombard (now Mrs. John T. Brush), and Mr. Jefferson's sons, Tom, Charlie, Joe, Jr., and Willie.

These good people were all seated around the dining-table of the special car that I entered, and the cordial greeting I received, combined with the contrast with "all-outdoors" and all else that had been depressing me, made me the happiest man on the continent. I remained there two or three hours, partly because, when manners suggested I should go, I was forcibly detained. I told stories whenever I could, but I was more entertained than entertaining. The time came when I was really obliged to go and I said:

"Mr. Jefferson, I am booked here to-night at a church, and I must begin my hour-long entertainment at seven o'clock."

"Well, Marshall," was the reply, "that will give you a chance to see our performance, so we'll reserve a box for you."

I thanked him, seized my bag, hurried to a hotel and prepared for my work. The church in which I appeared was crowded—packed, in fact; I afterward learned that, although I was well and properly paid, there had been no charge for admission. When I reached the theatre the house was only half full, but the performance of "The Rivals" was of full size. After the curtain fell I went to my hotel, packed my bag and hurried to the station; I had almost two hours to spare, but there are times when the station is more interesting than the hotel. Soon Charlie Jefferson stumbled over me and took me back to the company's car, where I had supper with the entire cast.

My train was due about an hour after midnight and as I rose to make my adieux, Mr. Jefferson looked kindly down on me, took me by the ear and said, in his own inimitable plaintive manner,

"I Seized My Bag and Hurried to a Hotel."

"Friends, I want you to look at this little scoundrel. He comes up here from New York; we entertain him; we dine him for three hours, he queers our house, yet gets a big fee for his own work. We again entertain him for hours by giving a "Rival" show, and yet he is not satisfied without taking my life"—with this he handed me a beautifully bound book, "Memoirs of Joseph Jefferson," with the inscription in the fly-leaf, "Presented to my little friend, Marshall P. Wilder."

Everybody tells stories of Jefferson's absent-mindedness, and he sometimes tells them himself. I can venture to repeat two which he himself has told. A friend of young Joe was making a long visit at Mr. Jefferson's house, so the comedian saw him at the table every day for a fortnight. One evening young Joe took his friend to the Player's Club, in New York. The elder Jefferson was there, and on being reminded of the young man's presence he said cordially,

"My boy, I'm very glad to meet you. Why don't you come up and see us? Do come and make me a visit."

But here is Jefferson's star story against himself.

"I was in a down-town office building in New York, a few years ago, and when I entered the elevator a short stout gentleman with a cigar in his fingers spoke to me, saying,

"'How do you do, Mr. Jefferson?'

"'I am very glad to see you,' I replied. He continued,

"'You don't know me, do you, Mr. Jefferson?'

"'Well, really, you must pardon me, but your face is quite familiar but your name has escaped my memory.'

"'My name is Grant,' he said quietly, with a twinkle in his eye. I got out at the next floor; I was so afraid I might ask him if he had been in the war."

But there is no accounting for absent-mindedness. Charles Wyndham, the English comedian, tells of an enthusiastic hunter, a man who thought of nothing else. One morning his wife saw him leaving the house and asked:

"Where are you going?"

"Hunting," was the reply.

"But where is your gun?"

"Bless me! I was sure I had left something behind."

Regarding sunny-hearted actors, it is well to remember that they too have troubles peculiarly their own, and one of the worst is to have an impulse where only solemnity is in order. Nat Goodwin who has been making audiences laugh for the last thirty years and I "took" a certain degree of masonry together, and as all masons know, the proceedings were quite as solemn as a church ceremony. Taking the degree with us was a worthy German, whose hold on the English language was both weak and spasmodic, as was manifested when it became our duty to repeat certain obligations, sentence or sentences after an officer of the lodge. Both Goodwin and I were fully impressed by the gravity of the occasion, yet we could not help hearing that German; he had a dialectic utterance that would have driven a Philadelphia vaudeville audience wild with delight and although he caught the sense of all the responses required of us, he unconsciously repeated many of them backward according to the constructive forms of the German language.

Goodwin and I knew it would be an unpardonable breach of decorum, as bad as laughing aloud in church in prayer time, if we gave way to our feelings. I bit my lips till they bled. Nat, less conventional, tried to stow his entire handkerchief in one side of his mouth, while he voiced the responses from the other. We had almost got full control of ourselves; the beautiful and impressive service was almost over, but when the oath was required, that engaging German repeated it backward. I yelled; Goodwin had a spasm—almost a fit.

To square ourselves, required a dinner for the entire lodge, and Goodwin and I were the hosts.

This was not the only scrape I was in with Nat Goodwin. During the bicycle craze of a few years ago, when wheels were as numerous at any good road-house as free-ticket beggars at a theatre, Nat and I met at the Casino, in McGowan's Pass, Central Park, and he asked me to wait for him, so that we might ride home together. We found many acquaintances about the tables, remained till after dark and then started homeward on bicycles without lamps. We had not expected to be out after sunset. At that time the law was very stringent and rightly so, about lights on bicycles, so I urged haste. Luckily I had many friends among the Park Police; they knew I was not a "scorcher" and that I had proper respect for my own life, so they kindly looked aside as we passed. But Nat—well they probably had seen him on the stage again and again and been the better for it, but actors don't wear their stage clothes and wigs and paint when they go bicycling, so none of the officers recognized him. At a turn of the road we came upon a policeman who didn't know me either, and he shouted—"Here you fellows—stop!" I don't believe I am a slippery chap, but I slipped past that officer before he could touch my wheel, but alas for poor Nat! he didn't. I did not remain to hear the conversation, for I knew I could not make any useful addition to it. Goodwin was to play the next night in Boston, so I expected to see a "scare head" story in the morning paper about his arrest. But fortunately while he was reasoning with the policeman, a friend came along in a carriage and succeeded in rescuing Nat and his bicycle from the clutches of the law.

I wish the carriage had been mine for Nat Goodwin has come to my rescue more than once. I recall one of the (London) Green-room Club's annual dinners, which Nat and I attended. It was given at the Crystal Palace; Mr. Bancroft—"Squire" Bancroft, "Squire" being his name and not a title—Mr. Bancroft was in the chair. About the middle of the evening a four cornered discussion between Sir Augustus Harris, Henry Arthur Jones, Henry Pettit and Comyns-Carr, all good fellows, became so heated that something had to be done to restore quiet, so Chairman Bancroft in a suave, diplomatic manner of which he has a mastery, arose and said,

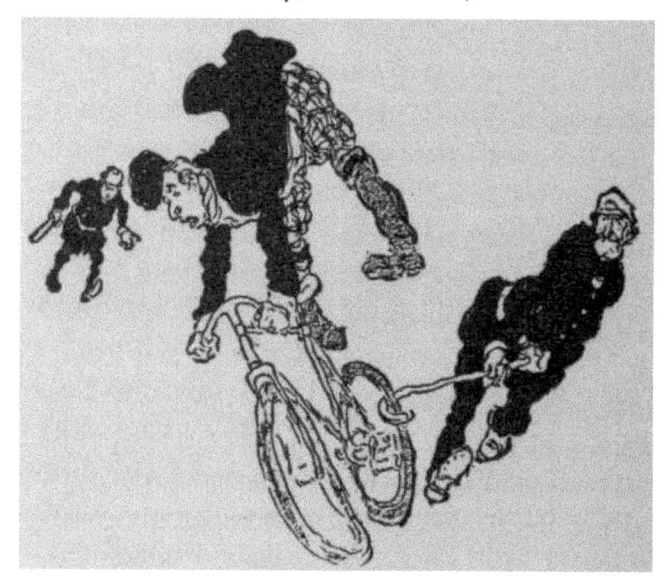

"I Slipped Past, But Alas for Poor Nat, He Didn't!"

"Gentlemen, we're here to-night for a good time. Let's quarrel to-morrow. I take great pleasure in calling upon our American friend, Mr. Marshall P. Wilder."

I arose, but the excitement had got all around the tables; my job was too big for me, and I could not raise a laugh.

As I dropped into my chair, the chairman called upon Mr. Goodwin. Nat got up; he began gently to spray oil on the troubled waters; then he drizzled it; showered it and finally poured it on by the tub full until he got the entire assemblage laughing and saved the day. I mean the night.

Some actors produce sunshine, that is, laughter, by direct means, others indirectly and by inversion. George Leslie and Wilton Lackaye are to the point, for Leslie is an optimist and "jollier," while Lackaye is sarcastic. One day Lackaye said to Leslie: "The only difference between you and me is that you bless people and things and I damn them—and neither of us is on the level."

At a dinner at the Lambs' Club, Lackaye bet Burr McIntosh that Burr would "make a break" nine times out of ten in whatever he did, and he added, "McIntosh, I'll let you select the times." It was amusing to hear Lackaye say, at the beginning of every dinner,—"Burr, that bet still goes." I believe it has not yet been decided.

But Lackaye is best when telling a joke against himself. While he was a member of the Daly Company, he said:

"Miss Ada Rehan is a charming lady, and I've always considered her a great comedienne—a creative one. At rehearsal one day we were standing aside and chatting, the scene not being ours and I asked off-hand,

"How Long Would it Take You to Like Me?"

"'Are you a quick study?'

"'Oh, yes, very,' she replied. I looked at her doubtingly and asked,

"'How long do you think it would take you to like me?'

"'Present?—or absent?' she asked. That floored me."

XXIV
SUNSHINE IS IN DEMAND

Laughter Wanted Everywhere.—Dismal Efforts at Fun.—English Humor.—The Difference Between Humor and Wit.—Composite Merriment.—Carefully Studied "Impromptus."—National Types of Humor.—Some Queer Substitutes for the Real Article.—Humor is Sometimes "Knocked Out," Yet Mirth is Medicine and Laughter Lengthens Life.

Perhaps the reason that the true jester is always sunny of heart and manner is that his output is always in demand. Busy though his wits and tongue may be, the demand always exceeds the supply. Laughter, like gold, is never a drug on the market, and, as is true regarding gold, people will endure some frightful substitutes rather than go without it. In countries that have no real fun in them—and there are such countries, the people insist on having laughter provided for them, even if they must depend on the public executioner to do it. It is said that in some Asiatic countries the people become wildly mirthful at the contortions of a criminal's body from which the head has just been severed; as to that, there are solemn Americans—men who would think it sinful to smile at a comedy, who almost split their sides with laughter over the floppings of a beheaded chicken.

"Split their sides with laughter over the flapping of a beheaded chicken."

As to that, I assert on my honor that I have seen Englishmen laugh over the pages of *Punch* and Frenchmen roused gleefully by a copy of *Le Petit*

Journal Pour Rire, though both papers seem as dismal, to the average American, as an old-fashioned German on the doom of the finally impenitent. According to competent judges the best thing that ever appeared in *Punch* was a poem on the death of Abraham Lincoln, which was not exactly a laughing matter. Yet the English are a good-natured people, and full of laughter. Sometimes it takes them a lot of time to get off a laugh, but, when the climax is really reached, the sound resembles an Indian war-whoop tangled up in a thunder-storm. They don't take their pleasure sadly, for there are no more cheery-faced people in the world, but their joke-makers are not successful when at work on serious subjects. *Punch* was never more popular than during the recent war in South Africa, when the greatest and best nation in Europe was being humiliated in plain sight of all the world by a few thousand Boers, not one in ten of whom ever fired a shot. It made me almost wish I could be an Englishman, just to see where the fun came in, for it was plain to see that it came.

But, to get back to my subject, every healthy man likes to laugh; therefore he likes whoever will make him laugh. Ella Wheeler Wilcox voiced a great truth when she wrote "Laugh, and the world laughs with you." Men are so fond of laughing that they will endure nine wormy chestnuts, badly served, if the tenth effort produces the genuine thing. Much of the best fun comes by accident; that is, from incongruity. Two of the few immortal figures of humorous literature—Don Quixote and Sancho Panza, owe their existence to this double motif; in the knight, by idealized chivalry being put down among pigs and kitchen wenches; while the persistent coarseness and vulgarity of his squire are thrown into juxtaposition with the chivalry and splendor of lords and ladies.

Every soul, man and woman, as well as many who are not, tries to provoke smiles, but not one in a thousand succeeds; as for those who actually create new humor, their name may be called on the fingers of two hands. Almost all humorists, whether amateur or professional, get no further than to evolve variations of old forms and climaxes, but what does it matter so long as they compel a laugh? At this sort of thing Americans beat the world. A cook who can serve a dozen different soups from one kettle is a bungler when compared with the American joker.

Mark Twain says there are only seven original jokes in existence and he ought to know, yet out of them has come an output that is incomparable, in proportion, except to the evolution of the entire English language, by varying the changes on the twenty-six letters of the alphabet.

The demand for laugh-making gives employment to many who might otherwise be in far worse business. These men are the founts of inspiration for the newspapers and the stage. The press and the footlights are ever clamoring for new fun and numberless are the attempts to supply the demand and incidentally utilize it in the form of cold cash. This stimulus has produced the humorist pure and simple, the paragrapher, the comic versifier, the compounder of burlesque and the maker of witty dialogue to spice the works of serious playwrights. There is also the humorous artist; when there isn't, there can always be found half a dozen tipsters who can't draw a line unless they have a yardstick to help them but who have enough funny concepts on tap (and for sale) to make fame and money for all the artists in the land.

The clever impromptu you hear in a vaudeville sketch, the delicious eight line dialogue you chuckle over in the morning paper, the flashing contest of wit you enjoy in a society drama often represent the labor, not of one but of a half dozen intellects trained to the elaboration of humorous conceits.

If all the humor which appears daily in print and on the stage could be clipped and put into scrap-books, it would fill forty large volumes in a year, yet nine-tenths of it—yes nine hundred and ninety-nine one thousandth would consist of variations of old facts, personalities, situations and plays upon words.

"The latest *jeux d'esprit* of Chinatown."

Besides all these clever fellows and their works, there are specialists in many other lines. Even a language serious enough in itself, may be so twisted as to make people laugh, especially if the twist can be nicknamed "dialect"; so we have the purveyor of German humor (so called) the manufacturer of

Irish "bulls," the sedlac of French jokes, the broker in Italian bon-mots, and a few days ago I heard of a cosmopolitan individual with a high sounding Celt-Iberian name, who offered to supply a prominent comedian with the latest humor of Portugal and Brazil. I don't doubt that before long some enterprising Mongolian will be trotting around among vaudeville managers with a stock of the latest *jeux d'esprit* of Chinatown, Canton, and Hong-kong, or that some one will put them in good enough shape to make people laugh. Good luck to them, for after all, the laugh is the thing. No one joke will be equally amusing to everybody, for each person has his own ideas of fun. For instance on a sunny Sunday afternoon in the country, a lot of good healthy minded folks will munch red winter apples and gather round the piano and sing "Happy Day," and other Sunday-school songs, and look as full of fun as any comedian's audience. And the grab-bag at the church fair! Around it there is more fun visible in human faces, than some great men get out of the cleverest jokes ever cracked. There is no end to fun, no more than there is to the melodies that keep rising, like birds from the eight keyed home of song, that octave that reaches from "Ta-ra-ra-boom-de-ay" to "Tannhäuser."

And there is no need of it all, for "mirth is medicine and laughter lengthens life." That is what my good friend Colonel Robert Ingersoll wrote under his picture which adorns my wall. The Colonel was one of us entertainers, though not professionally. Our merry champion he! The spirit of his tender epigram seems to haunt the dim twilight ways of men, looking with cheery solicitude for those who are weary, to take them by the hand and tell them tales full of dawn and breaking day, and rush of rosy life in rising sun. It stands on the side of light and love along the paths where flowers bloom and birds are glad in song. And it is needed, for from the start, there has been a fight between merriment and misery and the latter has its stout advocates. The gloomster and the jester have ever been sparring for paints and sometimes the jester has gone down under swinging right-handers; then, something that its enemies call Puritanism, probably because it hates all purity not of its own peculiar brand, has clapped its hands, all smeared with brimstone, until you could see the blue flames of the place that Ingersoll said didn't exist.

XXV
"BILL" NYE

A Humorist of the Best Sort.—Not True to His Own Description of Himself.—Everybody's Friend.—His Dog "Entomologist" and the Dog's Companions.—A Man With the Right Word for Every Occasion.—His Pen-Name was His Own.—Often Mistaken for a Distinguished Clergyman.—Killed by a Published Falsehood.

In one respect entertainers closely resemble preachers;—they greatly enjoy listening to the greater members of their own profession. Consequently, I never lost a chance to listen to Bill Nye, and I worship the memory of him as he was—a gentle yet sturdy and persistent humorist of so good a sort, that he never could help being humorous, no matter how uncongenial the surroundings. Although he saw hundreds and thousands of chances of hitting other men so hard that the hurt would last forever, he dropped every one of them and trampled them so hard that they never dared show their faces again. He was an apostle of the Golden Rule, which he exemplified in himself, so there never was a sting in his jokes; gentle raillery was the sweetest thing he ever attempted, and even this he did with so genial a smile and so merry an eye, that a word of his friendly chaffing was worth more than a cart-load of formal praise.

I speak what I do know, for he and I were close friends for many years before his untimely death, and he was so solicitous for my welfare and comfort, that after he had played father and mother to me successfully, he couldn't help going on till he had become my grandfather and grandmother, as well as a number of sisters and cousins and aunts.

I don't believe he ever had an enemy but himself, and he injured himself only by his peculiarities of self-description. Any one reading his humorous articles would imagine him an undersized scrawny backwoods invalid with an irritable disposition and an unquenchable thirst for something else than water. In reality he was a tall, broad-shouldered, deep-chested, healthy, genial chap so in love with the mere fact of living, that he took scrupulous care of himself in every way. He was as abstemious as any clergyman who is not a total abstainer, and he never lost his temper except when some deliberate scoundrelism was inflicted upon him. He would go out of his way—a whole day's journey out of his way, with all the railway fares and other discomforts in such cases made and provided,—to help a friend out of a sick bed or other trouble, and he endured all the torments of a busy entertainer's season on the road as cheerfully, as if he were perpetual holder of the record for patience.

People often wondered how he could go on year after year digging the same kind of fun out the same old vein, but the secret was that he lived right in the centre of that vein and was merely digging his way out of it. He had a full assortment of polite commonplaces, and carried them as gracefully as he did his full-dress clothes, but as soon as he got well acquainted with a man—and it didn't take him long to get inside of any decent fellow's waistcoat—he would talk in his characteristic droll manner all day and seven days a week, and as much longer as they two traveled together.

As seriously as if he were talking of audiences or hotel tables or railway nuisances, he told me a story of a dog he had owned. It was a Dachshund, and Nye described him as two and a-half dogs long by one dog high. He had named the animal "Entomologist," because it was a collector of insects. In fact, the dog lived up to his name so strenuously that something had to be done. A friend suggested soaking the dog in kerosene, saying,

"If it doesn't rid the dog of fleas, it will rid you of the dog."

So kerosene was tried and the dog passed away. After all was over Bill felt so bad that he went out for a walk, which did him no good. Returning home with dejected spirits and a sorrowing soul, he was smitten afresh with remorse when he realized that there would be no little dog awaiting him. But yes, surely there was something on the steps. Looking closer he saw seven hundred fleas sitting there, and they all looked up into his face as if to say,

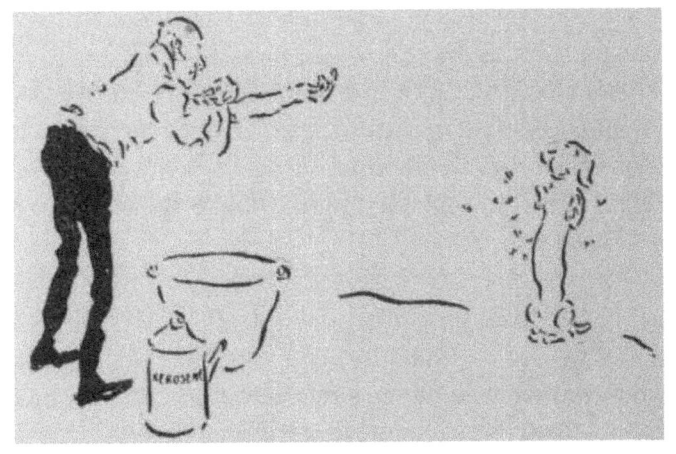

"He has named the animal 'Entomologist.'"

"When are you going to get us another dog?"

Few of the great world's great dispatches contained so much wisdom in so few words as Nye's historic wire from Washington—

"My friends and money gave out at 3 A. M."

He had an enviable faculty for suppressing annoyances in the course of an entertainment—something more dreaded by any entertainer than a thin house. In the course of one of his lectures in Minneapolis a late-comer had some difficulty about his seat, and lingered inside the inner door to voice some loud protestations. Of course every head in the audience turned toward the door;—anything for a change, no matter how good a thing has been provided.

Lingered inside the inner door to voice some loud protestations.

Nye endured the disturbance for some time; then he said politely but icily,

"This is a large auditorium, and a difficult one in which to hear, but fortunately we are provided with a speaker at each end of the house." It is needless to say which speaker received attention after that.

Mr. Nye was engaged to speak at Columbus, Ohio, in a newly-finished church with which the minister and his flock were as well pleased as a small boy with his first pair of trousers. So, in a short preliminary and self-congratulatory address the minister referred to the church edifice, called attention to its many details of architectural beauty and convenience, and laid special stress on its new and improved system of exits.

"Ladies and gentlemen," drawled Nye a moment later, "I have appeared in a great many cities, but this is the first time I have been preceded by any one instructing the audience how to get out."

Every man has his special trouble, but Nye had two; one was the reluctance of the public to believe that his pen name was his real name, and the other was the persistency of some people at mistaking for another fine fellow in a somewhat different public position—The Rev. Morgan Dix, D. D., LL. D., Rector of Trinity Parish, New York. Mr. Dix's stories are as good as his sermons, which is saying a great deal, and Nye's face when in repose suggested a man who could preach a strong sermon of his own. Nevertheless, it is awkward to be mistaken for any one but yourself. As to his name, every one who heard of Bill Nye associated him mentally with the oft-quoted person of the same name who first appeared in Bret Harte's poem "The Heathen Chinee," and assumed that the humorist's professional name was assumed. The poor chap explained at length, through a popular magazine, that he came honestly by his name, having been christened Edgar William Nye and nicknamed "Bill" from his cradle, but to his latest days he was besieged by autograph-hunters who asked for his signature—"your real name, too, please."

This genial man of cleanly life and good habits was brutally slaughtered by the public to whom for years he had given laughter and sunshine. People throughout the country turned against him when they heard the first breath of calumny. Without waiting to hear whether the story told of him was true or false, "The Dear Public" treated him so meanly that it crushed his spirit, sturdy, honest man though he was, broke his heart, and caused his death within a year.

It came about at Paterson, New Jersey, where he had been engaged to deliver a lecture. He had been suffering greatly from insomnia, for which expert medical direction he had taken a certain anodyne (non-alcoholic). Before his evening nap preceding the lecture he may have taken an overdose, or it may have worked slower than usual. Whatever the medical cause—for he had taken nothing else, he was drowsy and slow of speech on the platform. To make matters worse from the start, he tumbled over a loose edge of carpet as he came before the audience; although very near sighted, he had good professional precedents for disliking to wear glasses on the platform, otherwise his eyes might have saved his feet. But the succession of accident and manner impressed the audience wrongly. When the lecture was over some rough characters who had been in the audience followed Nye's carriage to the railway, throwing eggs at it and whooping like demons.

Next morning almost all the New York papers published the report that Mr. Nye had appeared before an audience the night before in an outrageously intoxicated condition, and had been egged off the platform! Newspapers are entirely at the mercy of the men whom they employ to collect news for them; some which used the Paterson story were honest enough to publish corrections afterward, but no correction is ever strong and swift enough to catch up with a lie. What I have said regarding the causeless cause of the untimely death of a humorist who can never be replaced is of my own knowledge; I was very close to Mr. Nye in the last year of his life and know what he thought and said.

I also had a strange reminder of the night on which the story started. Some of the audience had complained to the lecture committee that they had not received their money's worth, so it was decided to give another lecture without charge, to make amends for the disappointment. I chanced to be the man chosen to give the entertainment which was to apply salve to the wounded pockets of that audience, though I did not know it at the time. I did notice however, that the committee seemed to be "in a state of mind" and urged me to do my best. It also seemed to me that, metaphorically speaking, the entire audience had a chip on its shoulder; still, I succeeded in pleasing it.

After I had finished I learned that I had been selected to pacify the very people whose ignorance, stupidity and folly had caused the death of a good man who had been my friend. By a sad coincidence, it was on that very day that dear Bill Nye was buried!

XXVI
SOME SUNNY SOLDIERS

General Sherman.—His Dramatic Story of a Trysting-place.—The Battle of Shiloh Fought Anew.—Sherman and Barney Williams.—General Russell A. Alger On War.—General Lew Wallace.—The Room in Which He Wrote "Ben Hur."—His Donkey Story.—General Nelson A. Miles and Some of His Funny Stories.—A Father Who Wished He Had Been a Priest.

Soldiers are popularly supposed to be the grimmest men in the world, but I have found them a jolly lot, and the more prominent they were the greater the assortment of fun in them.

The first of the military profession whom I came to know well was General Sherman, and I never had a kindlier or cheerier friend. He had no end of good stories at his tongue's end, and no one cared if they were funny or serious when Sherman told them, for his manner was so earnest and animated that it was a treat to listen to him and look at him. Besides having a fluent tongue and a voice with no end of modulation, he talked also with his eyes and all his features, his head, hands and shoulders. It used to seem to me that a deaf man could understand all that Sherman was saying. He was one of the few talkers who could interest all sorts and conditions of hearers, from wise men and women, to simple boys and girls. Speaking of girls, reminds me of a story that General Sherman told one day at a dinner I attended with my friend Col. John A. Cockerill:

"When I was driving one day with General Grant, I asked him what he was going to have as a hobby, now that the war was over. He answered promptly, 'Horses,' and continued,

"'What's to be yours, Sherman?' and I replied,

"'Oh, I'll take the girls!' My fondness for the fair sex seems to be pretty well known, but I'm not ashamed of it; on the contrary, I'm very proud of it, for I don't know of any better company than nice girls of all ages—say from a hundred minutes to a hundred years. My fondness for them began early; why, when I was a mere boy I had a little sweetheart down South of whom I was very fond. We used to take long walks in the scented pine woods, and ride down the white 'pikes'; but our favorite spot—it became almost a trysting-place,—was a little hill on her father's plantation. No matter where we rode or walked, we were pretty sure to find our way to that spot, for it commanded a view of all the country round, yet it could scarcely be seen from the lower ground, for some pine-trees screened it.

"But this love idyl of mine came to naught, like many other boyish affairs. I went to West Point, the girl married another fellow and the next time I found myself in that part of the country was on the day of a desperate battle. The enemy was pressing us closely, we were contesting every step, yet losing ground, for lack of a good position for our batteries. Trees were so numerous that it seemed impossible to find a clearing or elevation from which the guns could be served to advantage.

"Suddenly, in spite of a head full of business and trouble, for my aides and other men's aides were bringing me dismal reports, and things were looking very dark, I realized where I was and remembered our beloved knoll. My mind's eye informed me that a more perfect position for field artillery could not have been designed, for it commanded the surrounding country to the full range of our guns. Yet for a moment I hesitated. It seemed desecration, for I had absolute reverence for the ground which that dear girl's feet had often pressed. But—yes, war *is* hell—my duty at the moment was to the nation, so I turned to an aide, described the knoll and told how the artillery could reach it. The batteries were soon in position there, and, as most of the enemy were in the open beyond the trees, they were quickly checked by a deadly fire, and we were saved."

This story was told as simply as I have repeated it, yet the manner of telling affected all the listeners noticeably. Colonel Cockerill leaned over me and whispered,

"I'm going to write that story up some day, Marshall, so you be careful to let it alone, and leave it to me."

I promised, but Cockerill's untimely death prevented him doing it. Besides, I have not attempted to "write it up."

Sherman's pen was quite as descriptive as his tongue, as the following letters to me will attest. One is on a subject on which he was very sore—the oft repeated story that on the first day of the battle of Pittsburg Landing, or Shiloh, our army was surprised and defeated.

"No. 75 West 71st St., New York, Jan. 1., 1890.

"Dear Marshall:—

"I thank you for sending me the printed paper containing the observations and experiences of our friend Cockerill about the battle of Shiloh or Pittsburg Landing, April 6 or 7, 1862. Having leisure this New Year's day, I have read every word of it, and from his standpoint as a boy, four miles from the war, where the hard fighting was done, his account was literally true. His father (a noble gentleman) and I were fighting for *time* because our enemy for the moment outnumbered us, and we had good reason to expect momentarily Lew Wallace's division, only six miles off, and Buell's whole army, only twenty miles away. By contesting every foot of ground, the enemy was checked till night. Our reinforcements came on the 7th. We swept our front and pursued a retreating enemy ten miles, and afterward followed up to Corinth, Memphis, Vicksburg, etc., etc., to the end. That bloody battle was fought April 6 and 7, 1862. After we had actually driven our assailants back to Corinth, twenty-six miles, we received the St. Louis, Cincinnati and Louisville papers, that we were 'surprised,' bayonetted in our beds (blankets on the ground) and disgracefully routed.

"These reports we heard at the river bank, and from steamboats under high pressure to get well away. And such is history.

"In the van of every battle is a train of fugitives. We had at the time 32,000 men, of which, say five or six thousand were at the steamboat landing, but what of the others? A braver, finer set of men never existed on earth. The reporters dwelt on the fugitives, because they were of them, but who is to stand up for the brave men at the front?

"We had no reporters with us. Like sensible men they preferred a steamboat bound for Paducah and Cincinnati, where they could describe the battle better than we, who were without pen and ink.

"This to me, is straw already threshed, for we had fought this battle on paper several times—a much more agreeable task than to fight with bullets.

"When in England some years ago, I was gratified to listen to old veterans fighting Waterloo and Sebastopol over again. So, I infer, our children will continue the fight of Shiloh long after we are dead and gone.

"Wishing you a Happy New Year, I am,

"Sincerely yours,

"W. T. SHERMAN."

"Preferred a Steamboat Bound for Paducah."

"75 W. 71st St., New York, Sept. 20, 1889.

"Marshall P. Wilder, Esq., The Alpine, New York City.

"MY DEAR MARSHALL:—

"I have now completed the first reading of the volume entitled, 'The People I've Smiled With,' and according to promise, write to assure you that it has afforded me unusual pleasure. I feel the better at having smiled with you, with enjoying many a happy laugh, and moved by its pathos; and as I infer you will have occasion to amend and add other volumes in the same strain, I venture to suggest, as to myself, page 211 should read, 'some years ago, down at the little village of Paducah, Ky., the Seventieth Ohio reported to me. Cockerill was a drummer boy in the regiment. His father was *the* colonel, and had got his education in Virginia, but was true to the nation. That regiment was with me at Shiloh, where we stood a heavy fire, and that is what made us staunch friends. He went ahead right straight along, as he has been doing ever since. As the sins of the father go down to the fourth generation, as the Bible says, it is a comfort to realize that the virtues go down *one*.'

"The stereotype plate can easily be changed to this, and it would be more accurate and satisfactory to military readers.

"Your anecdotes of after-dinner speakers, actors, actresses, etc., etc., are most interesting, and soon may become historic. I venture to add one which you can 'stow away' and use, or *not* according to your pleasure.

"In January, 1872, I was with my two aides, Colonel Anderson and Fred Grant, at the hotel Chauerain, Nice, when the servant brought me a card 'B. F. Williams, New York.' I answered 'show him up.' He soon entered my room, where I had a fire on the hearth, and for some minutes we talked about the weather, New York, etc.,—when he remarked: 'General

Sherman, I don't believe you recognize me. Possibly if I say I am *Barney Williams*, you will know me better.' Of course I did, and my greeting then was as hearty as he could have wished. He had called to invite me to a dinner party at his villa, which compliment I accepted for the next Sunday, and agreed upon the guests, including our minister, Mr. Washburn, then at Nice, James Watson Webb, Luther M. Kennet of St. Louis, and others, and a more distinguished or congenial company never assembled than did at that dinner. I must not, and will not attempt descriptions, even as to our witty genial host Barney Williams; all told stories of their personal experiences, and the veteran, James Watson Webb, in his grand and inimitable way, recounted his adventures when, in 1824, he was a lieutenant at Fort Dearborn (now Chicago). He traveled by night with a Sergeant of his Company, concealing himself by day, to Rock Island, to notify the Garrison that the Sioux and Foxes contemplated a surprise on their stockade on an occasion of a ball play, in which the Indians intended to massacre the whole garrison, which was prevented by this notice. But I now come to the real anecdote of Barney Williams. He narrated in his best style, his own early life as an actor: that in Dublin he was very poor, and took his meals at a cheap restaurant along with some fellows. Habitually they were waited on by a servant, most prompt and obliging, but who would periodically get on a bad spree. This occurred about the time when the Catholic priest, Father Matthews, was preaching the crusade against intemperance. These young actors conspired to cure this servant, and laid their plot. Paddy was absent several days, and their meals were served badly. At last he made his appearance, eyes bunged, face flushed, and the well-known symptoms of a big drunk. Whilst arranging the table for breakfast, Barney Williams read from the morning paper—'Horrible! Most Horrible! Last night as Terence O'Flanagan was lying on his bed, near which he had brought his candle, which he tried to blow out, the flames followed the fumes of the alcohol to his throat, and he died in terrible agony, etc., etc.'

"'What is that, sor? Please read it again,' said Paddy. It was read again with increased accent and additions. 'Please send for the Bible, mark on it the cross, and I will take the pledge.' The Bible was sent for and on it was marked the cross, when Paddy placed his hand on the book, and pronounced the pledge.

"Never as long as he lived, when on a drunk, would he attempt to blow out a candle. How far short of the reality seems the effect of words spoken or written. Therein comes the part of the drama, not the thing itself, but the nearest possible.

"I have seen Dioramas, Cycloramas, Dramas, Plays, etc., of war and its thousands of incidents. All fall short of the real thing; but I wish to be understood as not discouraging any honest effort to record the past, draw from it the lessons which make us wise and better, and still more, to give such as you, who make men, women and children happy and cheerful, when otherwise they might be moping and unhappy. God bless you!

"Sincerely your friend,

"W. T. SHERMAN."

A battle story seems natural to follow any mention of General Sherman, so here is one, given me one day, by General Russell A. Alger, Secretary of War in President McKinley's cabinet and also one of the best story-tellers in the Union. I have always been as curious as any other civilian regarding the feelings of a soldier going into battle and while he is fighting. General Alger told me one day that he could not describe it better than by repeating a little story. He said:

During a religious conference at Detroit four ministers were my guests. They, too, had wondered much about the sensations of the soldier in battle, and one of them asked me if I did not think the glory in taking part in great deeds, was a powerful stimulus causing soldiers to emulate the great heroes of history. I replied:

"Not at all."

Then they wanted to know what was the sentiment that took possession of the soldier when he was actually fighting. I replied that three words, only three, were frequently uttered by all classes of soldiers in the thick of a fight, and these words fully indicate the soldier's dominant sentiment.

In my division was a captain who was noted for religious life and extreme orthodoxy in belief and conduct. He was a strong Sabbatarian and had never been known to utter an oath, or even a mild word of the "cuss" variety. I regarded him as a Miss Nancy sort of man and feared he would be of no use in a battle, unless a quick and successful retreat might be necessary. But one day, while a big battle was going on, I saw right in the thickest of the fight, my mild mannered Captain waving his sword and urging his men on in such splendid style that I could not help admiring him! I rode up to compliment him, but when I got near him his language made me smile.

"Give 'em hell! Give 'em hell, boys!" he would yell after each volley—and he did not vary his remarks. I couldn't resist saying,

"Captain, I'm really surprised at such language from you,—you, our most religious soldier."

"Well, General," he replied, "I'm saying just what I feel, and just what I mean. Excuse me, but—business is business." Then he waved his sword again and repeated, "Give 'em hell, boys, give 'em hell—— Give 'em hell—— Give 'em hell," and gentlemen, those three words express the entire sentiment of a soldier while he is in battle! And, religious though they were, those three ministers looked as if they felt compelled to believe me.

One evening I stood at the landing of the grand staircase of General Alger's handsome residence at Detroit, looking down on a great social gathering on the floor below. Great men and charming women, elegant attires and animated faces combined to make a picture that I would not have missed for anything, but somehow my thoughts persisted in running in a contemplative groove, so I was not astonished when the general tapped me on the shoulder and rallied me on standing apart and being very quiet and serious. I replied, there were times when a professional funny man found it hard to live up to his reputation when he chanced to find himself alone and in a reflective mood. He not only understood me, but spoke most sympathetically of the necessary fluctuations of a mercurial temperament, and of the tendency of quicksilver to fall as quickly as it mounts.

Most truthfully did John G. Saxe, the humorous poet, write, "It's a very serious thing to be a funny man." Real fun must be spontaneous. The hostess who pounces upon me suddenly when the guests begin to yawn and exclaims imploringly, "Oh, Mr. Wilder! *Do* say something funny!" does not realize that she sends the mercury down with a rush.

Several times I have had the pleasure of meeting General Lew Wallace, the distinguished soldier, author and diplomat. He served his country gallantly in the Mexican War, when he was but twenty-one years of age, and afterward did inestimable service in the Civil War; he has been Governor of New Mexico, and American minister to Turkey, yet it is as the author of "Ben Hur" that he is most widely known and loved by his own country, as well as by Christian people of all nations, for his book has been translated into almost every European tongue.

When I was in New Mexico I visited the Spanish Palace at Santa Fé, which was General Wallace's residence during his governorship. The building was erected in 1598, long before the Pilgrim Fathers and Captain John Smith ever set foot on the Western Hemisphere, so it is one of the show places of the American Continent, yet the greatest interest of every visitor is the room in which "Ben Hur" was written.

Like every other real man of affairs, General Wallace has a large sunny side to his nature, and a gift for story-telling. I have listened to him with huge delight. To repeat all his stories good enough to print would crowd everything else out of my book, but here is one that I have often recalled, and with a hearty laugh each time:

In Stamboul, Turkey, lived a well-to-do native, named Ismail Hassan. He did not have the imagination of Rider Haggard or the eloquence of some Americans I could name, but he had a ready oriental wit that could always be trusted to get him out of a tight place. A neighbor called on him one day and wanted to borrow his donkey. Ismail made a low salaam and replied:

"Neighbor, I am very sorry, but my boy started on the donkey an hour ago for Scutari. By this time he is gaily trotting over the hills, far from the sacred precincts of Stamboul."

Just as Ismail finished speaking a loud bray was heard from the stable, which was under the same roof as the house. The neighbor exclaimed:

"How now, friend Ismail? I heard your donkey bray."

Ismail protested that the neighbor's ear had been deceived, and that the noise was not a donkey's bray. But the donkey, who was supposed to be trotting toward Scutari, brayed again, brayed twice, and loudly, so the neighbor cried,

"Surely that is your donkey, Ismail. Allah be praised, I can now borrow him." But Ismail replied angrily,

"Which do you believe is lying, the donkey or I?"

The neighbor could not set up the word of a donkey against that of Ismail Hassan, so he had to depart on foot.

"Who Is Lying, the Donkey or I?"

Although it has been my rare luck to meet many great and prominent men, I am frequently surprised anew that my first impression is of their simplicity of manner and their lack of affectation.

General Nelson A. Miles, until recently General-in-Chief of our Army, was always of distinguished appearance. In his earlier days he was known among the ladies in army circles as "Beauty Miles," and his photograph was in wild demand by young women at every military post in the west; yet he was always as modest and approachable as any ordinary mortal, and I am sure no American ever was more grateful for it than I, for I never outgrew my boyhood's adoration for soldiers.

I gratefully remember Miles calling on me once when I was in Washington. I ought to have been overcome by the honor, which certainly it was, but he disarmed embarrassment by "droppin' in" informally, head of the army though he was, in ordinary civilian costume and with an old soft hat on his head. On another occasion, when he chanced to be in New York, he saw me standing in front of "The Alpine," where I lived many years, stopped and chatted with me for a full half hour. As we were on Broadway, scores of men passed us every minute, and it was plain to see that many of them knew who he was and gazed at him respectfully and admiringly, yet no crowd collected and no one "rung in"; he was as little disturbed as if we had been in the middle of a ten acre lot. I was so delighted with the incident, with his manner and that of the people, that I asked him in what other country of the world the head of the army could be so unconventional and democratic.

"Well, Marsh," he replied, with a big smile of content, "that's the beauty of this country of ours—a man doesn't have to be anything but himself, or more than he wishes to be."

General Miles is loaded to the muzzle with good stories; he has so many that he tells them in as few words as possible, so as to have time to tell a lot of them. Here are some that he gave me one day in quick succession.

One Irishman bet another that he could drink a bottle of whiskey and not stagger. The other Irishman covered the bet, and the first one won, by going to bed and drinking the whiskey there.

A darky approached a fish stand kept by another darky and asked:

"Got any fresh fish?"

"'Cose I has. What you tink I'ze sellin'? Shoes?"

"Oh, I knows you's sellin' fish, but is dey fresh?"

"'Cose dey's fresh. Hyah!—quit smellin' o' dem fish!"

"I ain't smellin' 'em."

"What you doin', den?"

"I'ze jus' whisperin' to 'em: dat's all."

"An' what you whisperin' to dem fish?"

"Oh, I'ze jus' askin' 'em how's all dey're relations dat dey lef' in de ocean."

"An' what dey say?"

"Dey say it's so long since day seen 'em dat dey forgits."

An Irishman said: "Last night at two o'clock in the marnin' whin I was walkin' up and down the flure wid me bare feet on the oil-cloth wid a cryin' child on aich arm, I cuddent help rememberin' that me father wanted me to be a priest. But I thought I knew better than he did!"

XXVII
SOME FIRST EXPERIENCES

When I was a Boy.—One Christmas Frolic.—How I Got on One Theatre's Free List.—My First Experience as a Manager.—Strange Sequel of a Modest Business Effort.—My First Cigar and How It Undid Me.—The Only "Drink" I Ever Took.—My First Horse in Central Park.—I Volunteer as a Fifer in School Band, with Sad Results to All Concerned.

Senator Jones of Nevada, whose stories have greater influence than some other Senator's speeches, tells of a professional "repeater" who on election day voted early and late and often for the candidate of the party which had employed him, but who, just before the polls closed, begged permission to vote once the other ticket, which was that of his own party. With similar spirit I, who have been filling a book with mention of other people, want to record a few of my occasional doings. If some of these seem insignificant, I can only explain, in Shakespeare's words, "A poor thing, but mine own."

My memory goes back to the day I was baptized, but the first Christmas I can recall—and Christmas is the small boy's largest day, dawned when I was seven years old. My father and I had lived together as bachelors, so two aunts were the only mothers I ever knew. They lived at Wolcott, New York; together they owned a full dozen of children, and every boy and girl was healthy and full of fun. I always spent Christmas with them, and the first of these holidays I recall is still vivid in my mind, for I upset the whole town. My cousins and I exhausted our collective repertoires of mischief on the day before Christmas; children are usually "too serious." Suddenly I conceived the idea of disguising myself and discovering how it would feel to be somebody else.

So I blacked my face and in other ways hid my identity until even the family dog failed to recognize me. Then I practiced on several neighbors, not one of whom succeeded in seeing more than skin-deep. Thus encouraged, I called on a young lady of whom I was very fond—and let me remind my readers that a seven-year old boy's adoration is more whole-hearted, unselfish and intense than that of chaps who are from ten to twenty years older.

Well, I knocked at her door, after dark, intending to ask for something to eat. She herself opened the door, holding a lamp aloft, to see who the caller might be. Forgetting my disguise, I sprang toward her, after the manner of seven-year old lovers. She shrieked, dropped the lamp—which fortunately went out, and fled down several steps to the kitchen. Her cry of alarm startled a large bulldog, whose existence I had forgotten, but whose voice I recognized as he said distinctly, in dog lingo, "I'm after you." I took to my heels and ran homeward; he was handicapped by a door that had to be opened for him but I had barely got within my room door when he struck it with the impact of a cart-load of rocks and a roar which I can recall whenever I least want to.

"Struck it with the impact of a cart-load of rocks."

In my fright I confessed all and was sent to bed in disgrace. But I remained awake, for it was Christmas eve, and I had resolved to learn whether Santa Claus was the real thing. I got up at four o'clock, went down-stairs, but not a thing did I find. So I went back to bed, overslept, missed the prologue, and the others had the laugh on me. But I was round in time for the distribution of gifts, and as it was a case of twelve to one, all the cousins giving me presents, I felt that but for the dog incident I had got even with this first Christmas I can recall.

While I was a schoolboy at Rochester I was very fond of the theatre and used to "take in" every show that came to town. Generally this cost me nothing, although I was not on the manager's complimentary list. I would assist Janitor William Halloway light up old Corinthian Hall, where almost all attractions appeared; then after making a pretense of going home, I would conceal myself in the darkest part of the house I could find. This was easy to do, for I was very short; when the performance was about to begin I would bob up serenely, and no one would question me.

My first public appearance on any stage was back of our old house on North Fitzhugh Street, in a barn which my father never used. So some of my schoolmates and I turned the loft into a theatre. We rigged a stage with scenery and arranged for the lighting by making an opening in the roof. Pins were the only kind of currency accepted at the box-office, and I "in my time played many parts"; I would sell tickets at the lower door, keep children waiting to make them believe a great crowd was up-stairs, then I would hurry to the upper door, take the tickets and seat the holders wherever they would see best, if girls, where they would look best. My duties did not end here, for I was stage manager and appeared at every performance in various characters, so I honestly believe the audience got its money's worth.

My first business venture was in the peddling line; most boys have longings in that direction, but I was one of the few that persisted in spite of all opposition at home and elsewhere. I went from house to house with a basket of things which I was sure would be desired by housekeepers. The results were not as satisfactory as I had expected, housekeepers didn't really know how much they needed the articles I displayed and explained, yet I got some lessons that have made me a lifelong sympathizer with venders, book agents, canvassers, etc., for I recall distinctly the sensation of having doors closed in my face with some such remark as "Oh, get out of here; we don't want any."

On one occasion I rang the bell of a house on Thirty-fourth Street, near Park Avenue, New York. When the maid opened the door two lovely little girls peeped from the fold of her dress and exchanged wondering remarks about "the funny little man." I offered my wares; the maid said she would see the mistress. The little girls remained, we began to "make friends" and had reached the degree of confidence at which names and ages are compared. The maid returned to say that the mistress did not care to buy, but was sorry for me and had sent me a nickel. Being proud as well as poor, my impulse was to refuse the coin, but I put it in my pocket, saying I would keep it for luck (which it seemed to bring me). Years afterward at a Lambs' Club dinner a prominent judge said to me, "Mr. Wilder, I want you to meet my wife and daughters. Will you dine with us next Wednesday evening?"

I accepted, but when I climbed the steps of the house something compelled my memory to run backward and when I entered the drawing-room and was presented to the wife and charming daughters of my host it became clear to me that these were the kind-hearted people of long ago—the two little girls who had made friends with "the funny little man," and the good lady who was sorry for me and sent me a nickel.

I am not a smoker, but I did try a cigar once, and this first cigar is one of my lifelong memories. I encountered this cigar at a dinner given at the Hotel Astoria by the Aborigines Club. The decorations were appropriate in the extreme, the walls being hung with Indian blankets, war bonnets, bows and arrows and many other reminders of the noble red man. The central ornament of the large round table was a small Indian tepee, or tent, in which I, in the full regalia of an Indian brave, was stored before the guests arrived. At a signal given by Col. Tom Ochiltree, after the club and its guests were seated, I lighted a cigar; it was necessary for artistic verisimilitude that smoke could issue from the top of the tepee, and it would not be proper at the beginning of a dinner, for the smoke to be from anything not fragrant. Well, I never hesitated to try anything new, so the smoke went up, but soon afterward I went down—and out. The tepee began to dance; I felt smothered, and without waiting for the signal for my formal and stately appearance I threw open the flap, staggered about the table and saw the forty diners multiply into a hundred and fifty, all of whom engaged in erratic and fantastic gyrations. General Miles who was one of the guests, caught me as I was about to fall from the table. I was carried to another room and put to bed in a dejected state of mind and with a wet towel about my head. It was literally a case of "Lo, the poor Indian." Such is the history of my first, and—heaven help me—my last cigar.

"I threw open the flap and staggered about the table."

Although a total abstainer from spirituous liquors—for I can get as lively on cold water as any other man can on whiskey, I have to my credit or discredit, one single "drink." It was on a railway train, going from Liverpool to London, that I was tempted; unlike Adam and many drunkards, I cannot say "the woman tempted me," for it was a party of good fellows with whom I was traveling. As is generally known, European sleeping cars are divided into compartments—one for men and the other for women. Toward bedtime a flask of something stronger than water was passed— they called it "a nightcap"; all but I drank from it; I declined when invited, but when some one "dared" me to take a drink it was too much for my pride, so I yielded. There is a story of an Irishman who said to another,

"Have a drink, Moike?"

"No, Oi've just had wan."

"Well, have another. Ye can't fly wid wan wing."

I believed this assertion, for I was so exhausted by what I had swallowed that I soon made flying leaps from one berth to another and in other ways so conducted myself as to elicit shouts of laughter from the other men; our party became so noisy that the ladies in the next compartment got into a state of extreme indignation, rapped angrily on the wall, and sent the guard to us with frenzied appeals for silence. The effect of my physical condition was not so disastrous as that of my first cigar, but I caused as much disturbance as a man with a "load" which he should have made two trips for, and I was so grateful that matters were no worse that I resolved that my first drink should also be my last.

My first horse was another man's. On the site of Hammerstein's Theatre of Varieties used to be a stable, whose proprietor was so kind to me, when I was a New York schoolboy, that I used to spend much of my spare time there. He owned a little black mare which he allowed me to ride in Central Park. Her age and pedigree were unknown; some men said she had been in the Civil War; others dated her back to the Mexican War; she ought to have been in both for she was full of fighting blood, indicated by defiant waves of a little flag-like tail. I could not possibly fall off, for her back sloped into a natural cradle; her hips and shoulders would have made fine vantage points for wireless telegraphy. Her manner was distinguished by severe dignity, and her walk was slow and stately; nothing could urge her out of it, but occasionally of her own free will she would break into a decorous trot for two or three minutes. She was a capital illustration of Milton's idea of the female will:—

"When she will, she will, you may depend on't:

And when she won't she won't, and there's the end on't."

When she thought she had gone far enough she would calmly disregard any opinion I might have on the subject and return to the stable. I was much like the Irishman who drove a mule up and down a street, backward and forward, until a friend asked:

"I say, Moike, where are ye goin'?"

"How should I know? Ask the mule."

I must have been the cause of much amusement to beholders as I nestled in the depression of that animal's back. A facetious Park policeman once hailed me with,

"Say, young fellow? Why don't you get off and get inside?"

My first appearance as a musician was while I was in a primary school "annex" in the basement of a church which stood where the New Amsterdam Theatre now is. The teachers were so indulgent to me that I gave loose rein to my inclination toward practical joking, and I became an element of mischief which kept that school in a wild but constant ferment. One of the teachers planned a juvenile fife-and-drum corps and requested all boys who could perform on either instrument to step forward. I improved the opportunity to join the fifers, although I could not play a note. In time we made a creditable band; I stood next a boy who played well, and followed his motions industrially, though "faking" all the while. This went on a long time, to the huge delight of the boys who were in the secret; the teacher did not suspect me.

But the end came one day, in the presence of distinguished visitors. The fifers were few; the one I had imitated had remained at home, so I shook in my shoes when the corps was called on for music. The teacher, who was at the piano, missed the customary volume of sound, and looked searchingly at me. When she told me to stand beside her I knew my doom was sealed; I had never professed to be a soloist anyhow. But before I became officially dead I would have some more fun, and play the joke to the end. My short stature brought my instrument about to the level of the teacher's ear, from which position I let off at intervals a piercing blast which made that poor woman jump as if a wasp had stung her. I knew what was coming, after the visitors went, so beside having fun I was getting my revenge in advance. It is said that when Nemesis catches up with a man he feels her hand on his shoulder, but it was not on my shoulder that the hand of fate, represented by that teacher, was felt, for those were the good old days of corporal punishment in the public schools—the days when an offended teacher could flog a pupil as long as her strength lasted.

If these recollections do not please, at least I am at a safe distance, like the man who sent a poem in to Eugene Field, entitled, "Why Do I Live?" Field replied, "Because you sent your poem by mail."

www.ingramcontent.com/pod-product-compliance
Ingram Content Group UK Ltd.
Pitfield, Milton Keynes, MK11 3LW, UK
UKHW042148281224
453045UK00004B/237